After drinking from the mushroom cup, my tongue felt as if it were hibernating; I could barely mumble. "Forgive me. The journey must have tired me."

"The wine has made you drowsy," the fennec said.

"But I only drank one cup."

"It was a special kind of cup. A Death Cup."

"That's fatal," I said, not feeling the least bit imperiled. The words amused instead of alarmed me. "It . . . is . . . fatal."

"Not in the small quantity you have just imbibed. First you will sleep. You are—how old?—sixteen. Soon, an unsightly growth will deface your chin and cheeks. We shall save you from having to trim, perfume, or shave it. We shall *prevent* it. Your friend, however, is beyond redemption. It is more than a matter of excessive hair. He is too clumsy and too—*muscular*. But you—you shall soon be fit to associate with our Comelies without being troubled by their womanly sensualities.

"As for your friend, we are going to return him to his beast. The hyena has not been fed since his arrival. We shall test the extent of his affection for his master. How long will it be before he decides that appetite is stronger than devotion?"

Other ACE Books by Thomas Burnett Swann:

    LADY OF THE BEES

    THE TOURNAMENT OF THORNS

    THE WEIRWOODS

THOMAS BURNETT SWANN

MOONDUST

ace books
A Division of Charter Communications Inc.
A GROSSET & DUNLAP COMPANY
1120 Avenue of the Americas
New York, New York 10036

MOONDUST

Copyright © 1968 by Thomas Burnett Swann

An ACE Book

To Andy Morton,
Cousin incomparable,
Friend without peer.

Cover art by Stephen Hickman

Reprinted in 1977

Printed in U.S.A.

PART I:

The Peoples of the City

I

"Why should I let you live?" It was midnight in Joshua's tent. He loomed on a coarse straw mat which somehow his presence transformed into a dais; he was lit by the thorns and dung-cakes which blazed in the earthen hole, his hearth. He breathed the acrid air without coughing, attended by men less tall, who moved and coughed like human beings attending a god.

"Why should I let you live when you come from Jericho? Your city maintains an Egyptian garrison, pays tribute to the Pharaoh. My people have been at war with Egypt for more than forty years."

This Joshua of the Israelites was hard to answer. A mountain. A god. A mountain god like his one deity, the fabulous Yahweh who had led his countryman, Moses, out of Egypt, and led his own unkempt and unconquerable army across the Jordan to threaten Jericho. I had seen gods in images of clay, ivory, and bronze. Happy, human gods. The full-breasted lady of Crete with snakes in her hands. The shepherd god Shin of Jericho, who piped his flocks in the light of the moon, his home. But not like Joshua. His face was bearded so blackly and thickly that the individual hairs were lost in a fierce triangle of seeming stone. His eyes refused to blink and suspend their condemnations.

"I'm not a Jerichite."

"What have you to do with the woman called Rahab? You told my men you wished to free her from—what was the place?—Honey Heart."

"I'm her kinsman." His eyes burned me like thorns from his hearth. With my woodpecker-red hair, I resembled neither the swarthy Jerichites nor the fair Rahab. It was small wonder that I perplexed him. "But not by birth," I added feebly.

"How then?"

"By love."

"Is she your wife?" The question was not in the least absurd. At sixteen, I was thought to be ripe for marriage.

"She has been a sister to me. Closer than blood." I possessed few strengths in my little Cretan frame— not of hands nor feet, not to draw an Egyptian bow nor to ride a Hittite war charger. But I knew how to talk, even to a mountain. I knew how to talk, if only I could check the hot temper which often made me spit out words like sour pomegranate seeds.

"You asked if I were a Jerichite. No, I came there from Crete five years ago. With my parents and brother. I was eleven at the time. The great earthquake drove us from the island. My father, a merchant, lost his ships in a tidal wave and his house in a flow of lava. We sailed to Egypt with an Egyptian trader."

The mountain rumbled. Mention of Egypt, it seemed, risked earthquakes.

"There he had friends—he thought. They arranged

for him to take a post in Jericho. A minor post, to be sure, inspector of caravans. But what else could a merchant without ships expect?"

"What else indeed? So you came from Crete and settled in Jericho. But you have not told me yet about Rahab. Why you want to help her."

"I'm coming to Rahab," I said. "She is not to be come to without—dignity."

"No, she is not," he agreed with surprising readiness. I wondered what his spies, Salmon and Aram, had told him about her. Salmon had called her a heavenly visitant.

He did not interrupt me again. Once he clapped his hands and a dour woman appeared through the curtain behind him, scowling at me, smiling at him, and brought me goat's milk in the hollowed half of a coconut. The milk was warm and rancid but nevertheless welcome to one who had neither eaten nor drunk since leaving Jericho that morning. I began to speak with gestures and a certain grandiloquence, like an advocate arguing for a client before the thrice-royal Minos. I wanted Joshua's help. I wanted to win him with my eloquence. But I soon realized that such a man could only be won by the unadorned truth, even if it displeased him, presented in a simple narrative without flourishes. I became no more than the vessel of my story. Rahab was the wine.

Shortly after settling in Jericho, my father died from a demon of fever. My mother swore that the stench of pigs had killed him. She swore often through the next few years, though slightly under her breath lest she appear as uncouth as the Jerichites, and proceeded to

9

support us in that city of plague demons and people who deserved the plague by becoming a potter. She modeled her pots—that is to say, her vases, urns, cups, plates, and bowls—in the style she remembered from Crete. The joyful style. Dolphins frolicked through forests of anemones. Octopi coiled their tentacles with less ferocity than gaiety. True, the stream which watered the oasis of Jericho supplied inferior clay, and the river Jordan, five miles to the east, was out of reach for those like my mother who owned not even an ass, much less a camel, the new humped beast which some of the desert folk had begun to domesticate. True, also, she had to bake her pots on an open slab of stone, instead of in a kiln with separate shelves to control the heat.

"These aren't Cretan pots," she sighed, but the Jerichites, used to none half so fine, took them for rarities, and even King Akha's steward joined her customers. Surviving if not prospering, we lived in our two-room house astraddle the twin walls, we dressed in tunics as drab as the desert without sunlight, and we smelled the uninhibited stench of pigs, goats, and asses in a town where animals outnumbered men and surpassed them in manners.

Jerichite manners certainly did not extend to three Cretan exiles. Our red hair—Mother's fading, Ram's and mine foliating like palm fronds—branded us not only as foreigners, but as foreigners impossible to categorize.

"Red hair from Crete? But Cretans have black hair." It was the one fact which the Jerichites seemed to know about Crete, and they clung to it with the tenacity of an ass with a carrot.

"Most Cretans," Mother explained more times than she stoked her oven. She went on to explain that there

10

had been a time when our people had consorted with the demigods who inhabited our great forests. Thus, when you found a Cretan with pointed ears, you assumed a Faun in the woods of his ancestry, and a greenish tint to the hair suggested a Dryad in the family tree. In our own case, it seemed that the Woodpecker God, or one of his immediate offspring, the Red Tops, had mated with a mortal princess and we were the descendants, with hair the color of the red-crested woodpeckers which flash and flicker through the regions bordered by the Great Green Sea. My own name Bard, which had long been in the family—great-grandfather, uncle, and others—was either a corruption of "bird" or a reference to the fact that birds may be bards; that is, singers.

Mother's story was greeted with disdain, derision, or apathy. The Jerichites knew nothing of Fauns, Dryads, or Red Tops. Their own demigods tended to the demoniacal, and their gods, though amorous, preferred each other to mortals, at least to Jerichite mortals. The only person Mother convinced was an old lady with yellow hair (there was dye to be crushed from the almond nut), who snorted, "Well, of course I believe you. You look like woodpeckers, all three of you. Hopping about like birds gathering twigs! And small enough too, Shin knows." It was not a compliment but at least it was an affirmation.

Four years, rather like oxen turning a mill wheel, laboriously dragged us from our memories of Crete and Father. Mother grew old; I grew older but not, alas, up, except for a few inches; and Ram grew into a handsome and independent little boy of five whom neither my mother nor I deserved (unless loving can mean

11

deserving—in spite of my bad disposition, I loved him even when I was angriest with him)....

"Get your brother," Mother said, not looking up from the cup which she was burnishing to a high glaze, a rhyton shaped like the head of a snake goddess.

"Where is he?" I asked. I knew where he was. I was fighting for time, since I too was at work, modeling a fennec out of clay. At the moment he looked like his large red cousin, the fox. I had to endow his ears with greater than foxlike size in proportion to a smaller than foxlike body.

"Follow the pigs."

"Which pigs?"

"The dirtiest."

"But my—"

"Your fox can wait."

"It's a fennec, not a fox."

She had seen the animals often in the desert. She ought to know them from foxes. They did not so much emerge from their holes as explode, and then they withdrew so quickly that you felt as if you were still looking at them when it was their memory you saw, ears quivering to the sound of your approach, noses lifted to catch and interpret your scent. It was not shyness which made them skittish, but a sense of delicacy bordering on the fastidious. You were too large for them; gross, not dangerous.

"What's the difference?" It was Mother again, unwilling as usual to concede a point. "The desert makes them all look the same. Just as the town makes every living thing, man or beast, look like a pig. Rhadamanthus is well on his way."

Rhadamanthus—I called him Ram—was playing in the alley below our house. Most of Jericho's streets were alleys, and this particular one was neither wider nor cleaner than the rest, nor less frequented by animals. Ram's hair was so dusty that it looked gray instead of red, and from a distance I had the disquieting thought that he had turned into or been replaced by an aged dwarf. Changelings were not unknown in Jericho. I often had such thoughts about Ram. When someone is very precious, you rather expect to lose him, unless you have a god for an ally. I had yet to find a local god who convinced me of his powers.

As he came toward me, his young features showed through the aging dust. A sturdy little boy, his eyes the color of palm leaves, he was riding a large sow with rufous bristles. No battle horse could have been more proud of its rider, and no rider of his horse. He waved his hand—in greeting, I thought. No, he meant to warn me out of the way. The sow blinked and squinted her disagreeable eyes, which appeared to see little and dislike what they saw. I pressed my back against the wall and tried to further concentrate my small dimensions. The sow had room in which to avoid a collision, but she deliberately scraped against me as she passed and, at the same time, accidentally dislodged her rider. Somehow I caught him in my arms and fell, winded, to the ground.

The sow was slow to realize her loss. She grunted to a halt, twisted her almost neckless head over her heavy shoulders, and wheezed as she turned to glare at me. I was more than a little stunned, and my back ached cruelly from having been pressed against the rubbled surface of the wall. I returned her glare with

13

malice but without attempting, without feeling able to rise. Ram was her friend. He would be my hostage.

She heaved her heavy legs into a motion which soon became a gallop. Yes, that is the word. Walked or ran would not suggest her size, noise, and intention. She intended to trample her friend's captor and did not realize that she might also trample her friend.

Ram raised a hand and barked: *"Ariadne!"*

Aggression sank to docility, the gallop to a canter and then a lurch. She paused within smelling distance—she smelled of sour cheese—and awaited his command.

"You may let me go," he said.

I clutched him all the more tightly, and not as a hostage. I felt as if he might climb onto his sow and disappear for good, like a little boy in an old Cretan folktale my father had told me. In the tale, the boy had become a pig, and his brothers had looked for him in vain and finally been eaten by wolves.

"I said, you may let me go. I am quite safe." He was not rude. He never raised his voice to me, even when my disposition was at its worst. He was, however, adamant.

"She looks as if she would like to tusk me."

"Not now. She knows you're with me."

He reascended his mount, the sow submitting or rather shaping herself to his chubby legs, which were short even for his small frame. A less biddable mount could have dislodged him with a quiver.

"Would you like to lead Ariadne back to the house?" The sow could hardly have known that Ariadne had been a Cretan princess, famous for her beauty, but she must have liked the name, for she pricked her ears and blushed from dirt-and-pink to dirt-and-scarlet.

I knew that Ram's request was one of expedience. If he arrived in league with his older brother, he was less likely to be scolded for being late and for bringing home a sow; he could divide the blame.

"Honestly, Ram," I said. "I have to come looking for you in the gutter, and now you want me to lead your sow!"

"I couldn't let anyone else lead her."

Ram's requests, expedient or not, were impossible to deny. "Oh, very well. Climb back on." I suffered a reservation. "Do you think she'll tusk me?"

"Not unless you press too hard. Put your hand on her neck and ease her forward. That's right. She's getting to like you."

"How can you tell?"

"Because she hasn't tusked you."

To my surprise, her skin felt soft instead of leathery, and she glided under my touch without resistance, for Ram's sake no doubt, or because she could see at close range that my hair almost matched the color of her bristles. When we came to the stairs which climbed the wall, she started to balk, but the stairs climbed gently and even a sow with a boy on her back could negotiate the few inches between each step. I began to feel very proud of my little brother and his mount.

Our mother was waiting for us in the doorway, holding the edge of the sheepskin curtain in her hard brown hand. She was a woman in whom the Mother Goddess had exercised economy. Small, delicate bones; barely sufficient flesh to cover them; hair no longer worn in the Cretan style, a garden of curls, but swept from her forehead and caught at the nape of her neck by a simple band. Neither headdress, nor earrings, nor bracelets of

15

bone and ivory adorned her body. Even her robe, an earth-colored tunic falling to her sandals, was unornamented and ungirdled. Plain? No. There was a remnant of beauty about her, that of a conch shell bleached from its color but not yet broken from grace.

Though almost always fretful, she never displayed extremes of anger. She refused to waste the energy. Now she stared at us as if we were no more animate than the clay she molded into pots, and considerably less valuable. I could not bring myself to love her. Love was a word reserved for Ram, or for the girl I would meet if I ever left Jericho. Still, I remembered how she had been on Crete, bright and tranquil, the sea on a halcyon day. I might have loved her if she had appreciated Ram. But I noticed that other little boys, however dirty, had mothers who, however poor, brought them goats to pull their carts, or tunics colored like an oasis instead of a desert, and laughed as often as they scolded. There was something to be said for dirt; there was everything to be said for Ram.

"We can keep her on the roof," said Ram. "She's a stray," he added. "Needs a home."

Ignoring his request, she lifted him onto the ground and then examined her hands to see if she had soiled them. She sighed when she found no stains. She rather liked to find him as dirty as she expected.

"Shoo," she said to the sow. Ariadne ignored the dismissal. "What do you say to such animals? A Cretan pig would understand at once. But these Jerichite beasts—"

"We *could* keep her on the roof," I said. "Timnath next door keeps a goat. It sleeps on the roof with his children. We could heft Ariadne up our ladder."

"Pigs can't be 'hefted' up ladders," she said, authoritative on pigs as on other matters. "And I wish you wouldn't use those local barbarisms. 'Hefted' indeed!" All three of us had learned to speak Jerichite from necessity (or rather, Canaanite, a tongue which was widely spoken throughout the entire region between Egypt and Phoenicia), but Mother insisted that some words be left to the natives.

"*Shoo!*"

"But she's going to be eaten!" he wailed. "I heard an old man promise her hams to a butcher."

"So you stole her," said Mother frigidly. "She isn't a stray after all."

"Go home, Ariadne," Ram said, and the animal, whom I was beginning to like if only because she was Mother's exact opposite, fat and slovenly, padded along the wall and, settling hoof over hoof, descended into the alley and out of our lives. Ram gazed after her with wordless grief. Even at five, he knew the uselessness of tears. I put my arm around him and the gesture convinced our mother that we were in league against her.

"Sometimes," she snorted, "I wish I had daughters instead of sons." Surely the gods are listening when we make such wishes. Sometimes they take us at our word. "Come into the house now and get cleaned up for supper. We're having veal, dates, and cracknels."

The oven, which was no more than a wide, convex bowl of earthenware raised on stones and resting over a fire, glowed in readiness for the cracknels: honey cakes sprinkled with aromatic seeds.

"And what are you dawdling for?" she said to me when I paused at the worktable to look at my fennec. "You're almost as dirty as your brother." I started to follow him into the second room, which we shared with unsold pots, a cedar chest, and two pallets of neatly trimmed straw. Mother reached after me and caught hold of the sash which held my tunic.

"Wait a minute, Bard," she said. "I don't know why I'm so cross with you. You've worked as hard as I have today. Your fox is good. I expect you'll be able to sell him." She wiped her hands on a strip of linen, the last vestige of a gown she had brought from Crete, one of those billowing, bell-shaped gowns which the Cretan ladies wear when they wish to display their breasts. "I seem to be tired most of the time, and it makes me cross." There were moments, you see, when she remembered to be fond of us. The moments, I think, when she remembered Crete, and how she had walked beside the sea with a little parasol the color of hyacinths or ridden in a sedan-chair carried by two black slaves.

"It's because of the pots," I said. "You have to make so many of them. Why don't you rest tomorrow, Mother? Get out of the city for a change. They say the oleanders are blooming along the bank of the Moon Stream."

"Pink and white," she sighed. "Those are the colors I like best. We had them on Crete, remember? Better than oleanders, though. Roses! I sent a wreath to the Queen for the harvest festival. She wore them in the procession of the Goddess."

"You don't have to work every day, you know. I ought to finish my fennec tomorrow. That should buy you a day off!"

She gave an angry shrug. "We're both talking nonsense. You know I have to work. The King's chamberlain ordered three rhytons only yesterday. And your fox isn't even finished, much less sold." Then, with a

18

sigh: "Pots and pigs, pots and pigs. What else is there in this accursed town?"

There was something in the town which was truly accursed. But how could she know?

We sat on the floor around a large bowl in which there was a small amount of veal; we ate rapidly and noisily with our fingers. Mother did not scold us, she joined us. She was quite as hungry as her sons, and meat had become a luxury in Jericho. Though animals were plentiful, their owners were hoarding them—the edible kind—in case of a siege. Three hundred and fifty years ago, the wiry-bearded, slate-eyed Hyksos had captured the city from its original Canaanite rulers; a hundred and fifty years later, the Hyksos had yielded to the Egyptians, who were still our overlords. But the Egyptian garrison was small, the officers indolent, the men homesick for the pylons of Memphis and the obelisks of Thebes, and Egypt herself had suffered revolts and dissensions through the last forty years. A certain redoubtable Moses, whose exploits were so miraculous that some took him to be a god, was said to have led his people out of bondage in Egypt, aimed them at Canaan, and then ascended into heaven. The people, it seemed, were now on the move. South of the Dead Sea, caravans traveling between Tyre and Egypt had sighted an indeterminate number of very determined men, women, children, and animals who looked as if they had a destination.

For a few minutes after the meat, Mother allowed us to linger over the dates and cracknels. Then, as Ram was swallowing his last cracknel—

"Time to prepare the oven." Preparing the oven

19

meant exchanging the convex bowl for a flat slab, and I realized that Mother had let us rest only until the fire had died and the bowl had cooled. Early in the morning she would kindle another fire and bake her pots on the slab.

"I think I'll make a rhyton like a bull," she said, her voice softening again with nostalgia. "A Cretan bull. One from the Games."

I had never seen the Games. Before we left Crete, I had been too young for so deadly a sport. But I had seen the bulls in their pens, lithe, black, and electric, the earthly symbols of earth-shaking Zeus.

"It will be a lovely cup," I said.

Mother dismissed us into our room with a nod and began her preparations for bed. I could hear her through the curtain in the door: bathing from a pitcher and bowl (and after the heated showers of Crete!); leaving the house to empty the used water over the wall; returning and carefully fastening the hide curtain in the outer door. I stripped and lay on my straw, feeling it prickle through the robe I had stretched across its multiple sharpnesses. Ram lay across the room on a similar pallet. He was dimly visible in the glow of the hand-shaped clay lamp whose wick burned day and night, a deterrent to demons as well as a light for us. There was also a window, square now with moonlight, which looked down the city wall and the mound which lifted Jericho above the desert and, hopefully, above its enemies. I closed my eyes and crystallized Ram's features in my imagination. The green of his big eyes, the red of his hair, glittered in the black chamber of my brain: colors more sharp than in life because imagined, greener than malachites adorning the throat of a queen, redder than the carmine which painted her cheeks. Strange that tonight I saw him in feminine images. Perhaps I should say prophetic.

I fell asleep. I fell into the blackness of my brain (or perhaps the blackness fell out to encompass me). But not too quickly for me to think in spite of my fatigue: I should cling to the light—to the lamp and the moon. . . .

Jolted from sleep, I felt Ram climb into bed beside me.

"Fox," he mumbled. "Sharp teeth. Chasing me along wall."

"Foxes aren't big enough to hurt you. Must have been a wolf."

"Fox."

"Anyway, it was just a dream."

"No!"

"Well, he can't get in here. The window's more than thirty feet from the ground." I moved against the wall and made room for him, but soon I began to sweat and the straw pricked me like a hundred ant bites. The desert can be chilly at night, but our window did not even admit enough breeze to stir the lamp, and Ram's body was like a hot little bear cub nesting against me.

"Ram," I whispered. "Why don't we go on the roof where it's cool?"

"All right here," he murmured. "Fox fell off the wall."

It was not all right for me. I sweated on my back beside him, unable to recapture sleep and unwilling to try more comfortable positions for fear of waking him. The prospect of tomorrow, when I must carry Mother's pots to market at the city gate and bargain with the merchants, oppressed me more than the heat. Ram was not prone to nightmares; I doubted that the fox would return. Carefully I crept around him and made my way through Mother's room without waking her. She was always a heavy sleeper. "Why waste my rest?" she liked to say. "Work hard, sleep hard." I unfastened the curtain in the doorway, eased into the dark, and climbed the ladder onto the roof. I had made a nest of palm branches for just such nights. Here on the roof, above the stench of the town, the air smelled of dates, palm leaves, and olive boughs. Oasis scents. One could almost forget that Jericho had muddied the oasis as an island muddies a lake. . . .

I awoke to my mother's scream. It was not a scream for help; it seemed to say that it was too late for help. Thieves? Wolves from the desert? Splayfooted demons from the Underworld? I hesitated only long enough to break off the end of a palm branch for a weapon and half climbed, half tumbled down the ladder. Frantically I lifted the animalskin and paused to get my bearings. The room was dark except for Mother's lamp and the moonlight which came through the door behind me. I could see my mother crouched in the corner. I could see another shape, which I took to be Ram. Nothing moved. It was like looking into one of those dim Cretan caves where the worshipers are so still that you can hardly tell them from the sacred pillars to which they lift their arms.

"Mother," I cried, hesitating to let the curtain fall and extinguish the moonlight; waiting till someone spoke and told me the reason why a room appeared to have died, though nothing, it seemed, was lost or changed.

Slowly she raised her head. Her eyes were as dead as the room. "You left him alone."

"But he's all right, isn't he?"

"You went out and opened the curtain."

I yanked the curtain from the door and, swift as the flooding moonlight, crossed the room to my brother.

At first, I had seen what I expected to see; I had suffered a deception of the moon. I saw now that it was not my brother. It was a strange girl who looked as if she had lived in a cave or a tunnel and never seen the sun or played in the wind.

I seized her by the shoulders. She was not a child. She must have been almost my own age. "Who brought you here?" She felt like a jellyfish under my fingers; sticky and yielding. I wanted to hurt her into telling me the truth. I wanted to hurt her because her people had taken Ram.

"Don't touch her," my mother said. Her voice was far and passionless.

"But she knows where Ram has gone!"

"She will tell you nothing. She will taint you."

"But Ram—"

"It's too late to help him."

"But what *is* she?"

"Whatever she wants to be. Whatever they want her to be. A changeling."

I looked at her gray, shapeless face, puffy as if with bee stings. Only the eyes were beautiful. It was as if a clumsy child-god had molded her from rough-kneaded clay, but his divine mother had given her chrysoberyls for eyes.

"I don't think she can change herself," I said. "Else she would be beautiful all over. Like her eyes." Then

I thought that perhaps she could understand me and I had said a cruel thing. I patted her head to show that my fingers were not always hard. The hair was damp and lank. It was hard to be angry with such a pathetic creature. It was not she who had stolen my brother.

She flung her arms around me. I remembered that I was naked and froze with embarrassment. But she clung and clung and I yielded at last and gave her a tentative hug of reassurance.

My mother watched us with unutterable disgust. You would have thought that we were making love. "Tomorrow you will take her into the desert. Anyone can see she's one of its creatures."

I said with a firmness which surprised me, "I don't think we should do that. If we aren't kind to her, what will her people do to Ram?"

"He's ruined now. Like her."

"She didn't ask to be left here. I'll make her a bed on the roof. Or better, she can have my room."

My mother named her Rahab: The Wide One.

II

I HAD talked for perhaps an hour without interruption. In the smoky tent, my throat felt as if I had come through a sandstorm. At Joshua's signal the dour woman

24

returned to fill my cup with milk. In the midst of hostile or impassive males, I welcomed a female presence. Remember, I come from the island of the Great Mother. I smiled my gratitude. But she looked at me with such hostility that I hesitated to drink the milk for fear of poison. Swathed in black robes, with black ringlets of hair escaping from a black headdress, she resembled an irritable raven. I was not to be intimidated. I scorched her with the look I reserve for someone who tries to shortchange me in the marketplace. Uncowed, she flapped from the room.

Joshua had noticed our exchange of look. "Do not mind Reshel. To her, every one from Jericho is a demon. She has heard that you sacrifice babies to Astarte." He paused. "Do you?"

"Only with the parents' permission."

"You were telling me about the changeling left in place of your brother. You called her Rahab, and you said that she was *ugly?*" He sounded incredulous, almost accusing.

At the time, yes. She was ugly by all human standards of grace, symmetry, and coloring. Except for her eyes, which burned in her pallid face like embers in ashes. Other girls might cry. Not Rahab. The anguish in her eyes was beyond tears. Only she knew how much she had lost, but both of us knew how little she had found.

She never spoke. Perhaps she was mute, I thought. Perhaps her people did not know Canaanite. But she did not need to speak. She listened and looked her understanding when I talked about Ram.

"Ram would have liked this pig I'm modeling," I

might say. Or, "Ram would disapprove of this cat. He never much liked cats. Too clean." She would nod and smile and look much older than her years. It was as if her eyes remembered him.

From first to last my mother despised the girl. She had named her Rahab as a cruel jest, and she treated her with indifference or spite. It was not so much that she missed Ram, but that she felt victimized, as if she had labored a year to bake vases and then had them stolen from her. Ram had been stolen. It was unjust; more than that, it was wicked. She was outraged with the demons who had taken him and the gods who had allowed him to be taken. She was outraged with Rahab for having taken his place. She continued to keep the house with her usual thoroughness, but her motions became lethargic and heavy, like those of a person who has sipped of hemlock. She stopped making vases. She stopped going to the market.

I was the potter now, but instead of pots I molded animals—bears, foxes, camels—which sold surprisingly well and brought us clay for the oven, food for the table, and silvers to pay in taxes to King Akha, who paid them in turn to support the Egyptian garrison. The cloddish Jerichites were used to artists—artisans, I should say—who distinguished a pig from a dog only by making him fat. My animals resembled their models. My pigs were porcine from their curly tails to their flat snouts. . . .

Events accumulated into a year. Rahab was silent but loving; Mother, silent and beyond love. To me, the events were not in themselves important except that they melted time, much as the Jordan melts its banks. I was glad to lose time; to see it flowing behind me like muddied waters. Time without Ram was better lost. It was modeling animals for love but selling them for money. It was the coming of caravans out of Egypt and bound for Sidon or Tyre. It was the gossip in the marketplace: "Horde your grain, husband your animals. The Wanderers are on the move. Numerous as locusts, and just as hungry!"

Even when Mother died, I did not feel that the event was extraordinary. She had become a presence and not a person. It was inevitable and predictable that the gods would demand the soul which she held so carelessly. Her death, like her life, was neat and circumspect. One morning when I overslept and clambered down from the roof so as not to miss my breakfast, I found her, eyes open, looking as if she had finished sweeping the house; not exactly pleased—nothing so positive—but quietly satisfied. I knew at once that she was dead. She never slept after cockcrow hour. I sat down beside her pallet and took her hand, but I had no wish to recall her to a world she would not miss. I thought of her journey to the Underworld where the Griffin Judge stands guard at the portals of the Amber Palace. He would judge her kindly, I hoped; as a Cretan and not as an exile. He would let her pass into the halls of the Great Mother. There would be tall columns swelling into capitals like pomegranates; there would be a throne of gypsum in a room whose frescoes laughed with dolphins and leaped with flying fish. And lightwells brimming with sun. And the music of lyres and sistrums. Whatever my mother had lost when she left Crete.

When I began to cry, it was not really for her, but for Ram. In losing her I had lost the last person who had shared him with me. I stretched on the floor, pressed my face against the cold, burnished limestone, and cried so bitterly that I did not hear Rahab come into the room.

She sat down beside me and spoke in perfect, if hesitant, Canaanite: "Don't be sad."

I gazed at her with astonishment. "You can speak."

"I've understood you for some time. Now I can answer you."

"How did you learn?"

She looked puzzled. "I don't think I learned. It's as if I knew a long time ago but forgot. Now I seem to be remembering. When I spoke to you then, I had only meant to touch your hand. But the words came of themselves. You see, I'm a little afraid to touch you. I hesitated—and my tongue remembered and saved me the embarrassment."

"You needn't be embarrassed. You're like my own sister!"

"Even a sister should have pretty fingers." She was wearing a brown tunic which reached to her ankles. She always covered as much of herself as possible. There was no border in gold or silver thread; she wore neither bracelets nor anklets. Had she been plain instead of ugly, the robe might have effaced her from the surroundings—made her no more noticeable than a bench or a couch. As it was, her ugliness attracted stares wherever she went. Women in the Fountain House gazed disdainfully at the limp, straight hair—was it brown or had it a color at all?—which no headdress could quite contain. Men made jokes in the marketplace about the thick, shapeless body which no tunic could hide.

"Have you remembered anything else? About Ram?"

"No. I don't even know who brought me here. Or

28

who took him away. Sometimes—do you think this is strange?—I seem to be walking among giant mushrooms. Or else I'm flying in an orange sky with moths as big as griffins. And there are beings on the ground watching me. Some are people, and some are—I want to say dwarfs, but that doesn't quite describe them, except that they're small and brown."

"Are they kind?"

"Kind? I don't know. I'm not sure that they concern themselves with words like kindness and cruelty. I seem to belong with them, though. I do know that."

"Is Ram with them?"

She frowned. "I hope not. He doesn't belong. Not from what you've told me. The moths have mandibles like daggers. But we must see to your mother, mustn't we?"

I flushed with shame at having forgotten her. The wonder of Rahab's speech had distracted me from my duties to the dead. I knelt beside her and studied the features which in life had worn a mask of disapproval. She looked younger than I remembered, almost beautiful now that the scorn and impatience had left her face.

"Your mother disliked me from the first. But I never disliked her."

"I don't think she very much noticed either of us."

"She noticed me. She was always afraid I was going to break something. I look so clumsy. Did you love her, Bard?"

"I was used to her. Fond of her."

"And now there's nobody you're used to. I'll try to become—familiar. Do you think I ever can? Looking this way, I mean?"

"Looking what way?"

29

"Not like other girls. White when they're brown. Flabby when they're soft. Uncomely."

"You look fine to me."

She smiled. "I must be becoming familiar."

After her death, my mother's tidy house became a jungle, with Rahab and me its keepers. The smell of clay made you think of riverbanks in the sun; vats of dye glittered like bright-winged phoenixes, and the drops which splattered to the floor might have been escaping feathers. There was the oven, and a bench of aspen wood on four tall legs, and a table for modeling, and a pallet of palm fronds. Everywhere else were animals. Not only baking on the oven or drying on the table, but crouched, sprawled, and skulking over the floor, lurking in the corners, abiding on either side of the door. Animals such as lived in Jericho or the adjacent desert: fox and pig and fennec. Animals such as I had never seen: hippogriph and phoenix and hippocampus. And animals such as I invented: the birdobear, with the body of a bear and the wings of a seagull. In the morning I molded and baked with Rahab's help. In the afternoon, while Rahab sifted, combed, and spun flax to make our coverlets and robes, I went into the marketplace to sell my creations. In the evening, Rahab and I counted our silvers and decided how many animals we could keep and how many we would have to sell.

"You must keep the birdobear," she would say. "I'll spin you a new tunic and you won't have to buy one. We can count five silvers as saved."

Familiarity is one of the faces of love. . . .

It was the morning of my sixteenth birthday.

Rahab said: "Let's get out of the city." Her usually pallid cheeks were flushed from her walk. She was holding a basket woven from reeds. "You see, I've been to the market." Trips to the market were rare for her, alone or with me. She disliked the stares and hated the merchants who tried to sell her ornaments and mirrors.

"I can't," I said. "I have to finish my wolf." I had never seen an actual wolf, but Rahab had given me excellent advice. Elongate his tail ("not like a bear's —it has to be able to lash"). Remove his mane ("you're making him look like a lion"). He was almost ready to be dyed with umber from the banks of the Moon Stream.

"Except for the dye, he's finished," she said. "If you keep on smoothing him, he'll lose his ruggedness. Wolves are meant to look fierce. You certainly have time for a picnic on your birthday."

"Sixteen," I sighed. "Old enough to bear arms if the Wanderers cross the Jordan."

"How can they cross the Jordan? It's flooded with melting snow. Some of the men can swim across, but not the women and children. They're not just an army, they're an exodus. They need another miracle."

"If they want to cross, they'll find a way." I had never seen the Wanderers, though I felt that I knew them from the reports of travelers. Silent, indomitable, and irresistible. A human flood more terrible than the Jordan. I admired them immensely. Jericho could use a flood to clean its human refuse.

"You're putting me off." She took my hand and thrust it into the basket. "Cracknels," she said. "And figs."

I winced. Ram had loved cracknels and figs. I busied myself with the wolf. "Out of the question."

Rahab was usually biddable. Today she was unusual. "I'll go alone."

"Girls get ravished alone. Some of the Wanderers may have swum the Jordan."

"Then I'll get ravished by a Wanderer. At least he'll be clean after his swim."

I set the wolf down so hard that I broke his leg. For a girl who had never been kissed, or even looked at by someone who wanted to kiss her, Rahab could make some worldly remarks. "Very well. I'll go on a picnic with you and lose a whole day of work and have nothing to sell tomorrow in the market. Then what will we do for silvers to buy you a new robe?"

"A new robe isn't going to make me beautiful." She handed me the basket. The reeds felt cool in my hands. I knew that they had come from the banks of the Moon Stream, which flowed under the city and out into the oasis, filled our irrigation ditches, and watered our vineyards and grainfields. They rustled of palm trees instead of people and what it was like to play instead of work. Perhaps we would see a caravan from Egypt, a procession of asses—even a camel or two—laden with amethysts and unguents, ebony jewel caskets and silver mirrors. My thoughts meandered like the Moon Stream. Clear waters to wade in . . . acacias to lie in . . . sunlight filtered by palm leaves to an amber shade.

"All right," I said. "But just for the morning."

In the heart of Jericho, one felt imprisoned as if in a great city like Knossos or Thebes. The fifteen hundred Jerichites, crowded into less than six acres of close-built temples and houses, appeared to be as limitless as the Wanderers. There was no alley without its goats and pigs; there was scarcely an alley without its men and women, afoot or on ass-back. I will have to say for the animals that most of them were well-fed, even if offensive; and for the people that prosperity became their bodies—smooth, sleek, and garbed in multicolored linens—if not their miserly hearts. But walking among them was to endure stenches, jostlings, and stares, and passing through the city gate was to bathe in air and sunshine. The guard at the gate, an Egyptian with loincloth and bare shoulders, let us pass without question. Only at night, when the farmers and the shepherds had come from the fields, did the guards close the gate and shut the town within the presumed impregnability of her walls.

The marketplace, too large for the tortuous confines of the city, clustered around the gate as if to borrow its security even while enjoying the freedom of the oasis. With its myriad canvas stalls—blue, red, yellow—winking in the sun, it looked like a camp of lighthearted desert dwellers. But its merchants were light of heart only when they anticipated or concluded a sale. They brightened to duty as we approached, vaunted the freshness of their peppercorns or the sturdiness of their pots, and sank into heavy-lidded torpor when we had passed.

One man called after me, "Boy, would you care to buy a veil for your friend?"

Anger bubbled in me like lava. I spun in my tracks to confront a row of expressionless eyes in fat, sun-reddened faces. I could not tell who had spoken, and no one ventured to identify him.

Rahab touched my arm. "Come on, Bard. He meant no harm. You know what they say about veils: 'To a pretty woman, an affront. To a plain woman, a friend.' "

Jericho looked redoubtable from the distance of half a mile. Its double walls, thirty feet tall, the inner one twelve feet thick, the outer one six feet, seemed an unbroken and unbreakable barrier instead of innumerable porous bricks with cracks between them and with heavy houses weighing them down on their uncertain foundations. It was like a huge orange toadstool sprouted by the fertile oasis. You admired its color and its contours. Only when you remembered the flaws did you wonder if the kick of a giant could burst it and scatter its fragments to the sand-sharp winds.

We stopped near the edge of the oasis, where the Moon Stream flowed among thickets whose seven-foot papyruses harbored the heron and the pintail duck. Both the plants and the birds had been imported from Egypt—from the marshlands along the Nile—by a homesick garrison.

"There's too much of Egypt in Jericho," said Rahab. I knew she was thinking about the Pharaoh's cruelty to the Wanderers. "I don't even like Egyptian plants."

We sat down in a clump of indigenous acacias, yellowing with the spring into fluffy balls of close-clustering blossoms. The feathery leaves mellowed the glare of the sun. We could hear the sounds of the city—human voices and animal bleatings—but distance gave them the music and unreality of sheep bells heard in a meadow. The stream, invisible from where we sat, rustled silverly between its banks and seemed to wash the air as well as the earth. A heron arrowed above our heads, a slender ivory shaft. Only he had the right to a sky so washed and pure.

I looked at Rahab as she unfolded our lunch from its linen wrappings. Even the leaf-filtered sun was cruel to her features. The flush I had seen when she returned from the marketplace had remained and deepened until it seemed the red of fever instead of health, and her usually slack skin looked tight and hard.

"I thought you were used to me," she said.

"I didn't mean to stare. It's just that you don't look well."

She shrugged. "It's spring. People are making love. I haven't a face anyone would want to look at, much less touch. That's my illness. I'm afraid it's incurable."

"Do you want to look like those stupid Jerichite girls? Sleek and cow-eyed?"

"There's something to be said for cows. At least they attract bulls."

A boy and a girl, fused rather than embraced, burst out of the acacias and stared at us as if we had stolen their trysting place. The boy's loincloth was brief to the point of indecency; he might have been a bull wrestler from Knossos, stripped for the games. The girl had lost her sash and was about to lose her robe. They left us with a simultaneous shrug and apparently found a spot to their liking up the stream. Their splashes grew frenetic. With the cruel clarity of my imagination I watched them disrobe and disport until I felt like a peeper and blinked my eyes.

"You ought to have a girl," Rahab said. "You're sixteen. Old enough for a wife."

"I have you," I said sharply.

"I'm your sister. You know what I mean."

"You want me to be like that boy we just saw? He's disgusting. Both of them are."

"Stupid, perhaps. Disgusting, no. The Mother Goddess has told them to multiply."

"What has the Mother Goddess to do with them? Not our Cretan Mother, at any rate. They lust for each other, that's all. They're animals."

"They're beautiful to each other. Whatever they do seems sacred. I would like to be that girl."

"No, you wouldn't," I said firmly. "When the time comes for you to marry, you'll go about it in the proper way. I'll speak to the boy's father before you do any holding hands. And you won't marry a Jerichite."

"Bard, you're a prude. Quite unlike your countrymen, from all I've heard. Do you know why?"

"In the first place, I don't think I'm a prude. In the second place, I would rather be a prude than a lecher."

Gentle Rahab had never been more persistent. "Because you're a passionate boy without a girl. That's why. Lovers make you angry because you envy them."

"Open the lunch," I snapped.

"I like to see you angry. Even at me. You seem to catch fire. Green eyes and red hair. A double flame. You're quite handsome, you know."

"All five feet of me."

"You told me yourself that's the average height for a Cretan male."

"We're not in Crete. I suffer in comparison to the natives."

"Not in comparison to me. I'm less than that myself."

"You're a girl. Eat a cracknel."

Then I saw the fennec.

Where the lovers had parted the acacias, he sat on his haunches and watched us with benign dignity. Smaller than the fox, his cousin, he was about the size of a cat. His black-tipped tail quivered with expectation. His small black eyes blinked with intelligence.

His immense, papyrus-thin ears, an insult to any other animal, became him. I wondered why Rahab was not surprised. As far as I knew, the only fennec she had ever seen was the model in my shop.

"Stroke him," she said. "But here, wipe your hands first on this linen. There now. Don't go against his fur."

He tensed under my fingers; he had to decide if I were patronizing or honoring him. He began to purr.

"We must take him home with us," Rahab said.

"They are desert creatures," I protested. "I've never known one to live in captivity."

"I didn't say captivity. I said we must take him home with us." Her voice sounded raw and almost shrill. I should have been warned.

"It's out of the question. What would we feed him? There's hardly enough for us."

"You hate me," she cried. "You hate me because I'm ugly and I took your brother's place!"

She sprang to her feet and groped through the acacias, thrusting apart the leaves with spasmodic bursts of her hands. It was as if she were clawing a path through spider webs.

I overtook her beside the stream. Her skin looked blotched and cracked. She tried to push me away but her hands fell limply between us like dying butterflies.

"Of course you can take him home," I cried. "Of course you can take him home."

I caught her shoulders between my hands and kept her from falling when she closed her eyes. I lifted her in my arms and stumbled toward Jericho; I might have been lifting a corpse.

The fennec kept pace with me.

III

She stirred as I placed her on the pallet; she writhed into consciousness. Her face was monstrous. The cracks had become wounds. She seemed to be disintegrating before my eyes. She began to claw at her robe with desperate fingers.

"I can't breathe," she whispered. "My flesh is suffocating me."

I helped her remove the constricting tunic. Her body bulged and heaved beneath the thin linen of her undergarment. She looked like a woman in childbirth.

"Demons," she said. "I think they're taking my body."

"Fight them!"

"Let them have it. It's nothing to me."

"No!"

"What can I do?"

"I'll get a holy man!"

On Crete, we had physicians to fight the demons of sickness. In Jericho, it was the temple priests who fought them, with imprecations, images, and potions.

I rose from the pallet and spun toward the door.

"Bard," she said. Her voice might have come from the bottom of a well.

"Yes."

"I love you."

I fled onto the wall and floundered down the stairs into the street. I overturned a cart of coconuts and sent a goat careening into a crowd of gossipers, who proceeded to pelt me with the coconuts.

A woman barred my path, laughing brazenly. The ring in her nose and excess of kohl around her eyes marked her as a prostitute. Such women always annoyed me; this one, at such a time, infuriated me.

She caught my arm. Her fingers felt like pincers. "Red Top. Where are you running? Away from a husband or to your girl?"

"To a temple priest," I scowled. "I have leprosy."

I left her frantically washing her hands in the milk of a coconut.

The temple of Shin, the moon god and patron of shepherds, belonged in Knossos instead of Jericho. Its blue-bricked facade, set among buildings of monotonous brown, was a corner of sky fallen to the earth, a corner of peace in a dusty chaos. Its sanctuary was sweet with burning frankincense and the gum of rock roses. The clay image of the god dreamed on its wooden pedestal. I guessed the crudity of its modeling, the garishness of its paint, but in the twilight of the incense burners, the image became the god, slim as a young cedar, extending his arms with a benediction of moonlight. Five worshipers—shepherds, to judge from their sheepskins—surrounded the image with open mouths and with hands raised above their heads in prayer. A priest was chanting:

"Shin,
Moonborn,

39

Moonbright,
Guardian of herds in the copper mountains:
May the ewes suckle their lambs
In the light of your sky-far home. . . ."

I committed a minor sacrilege. I interrupted the prayer. "Please," I said. "My sister is possessed by demons. Can you heal her?"

The priest of the goddess Astarte, the Jerichite perversion of the Mother Goddess, would probably have ordered my imprisonment. The priest of Shin, however, continued his chant:

"And the shepherds walk tall among wolves . . ."

But he motioned with his hand to a door in the rear of the sanctuary as if to say: Someone beyond the door will help you.

I found myself in a courtyard enclosed by a high brick wall. There were palm trees, and pools aflutter with blue lotuses, and oleanders trailing their long leaves like questing fingers. And animals: Sleeping in roofless pens under the palms. Drinking from the pools. Grazing beside the paths. A sheep with a leg in a splint. An ostrich blindfolded—or perhaps bandaged—with a woman's veil. A camel with a patch over one of his eyes.

A hairy young man, wearing a disheveled purple tunic which reached halfway from his thighs to his knees, sat by the pool and trailed his feet in the water. In his arms he held a small lamb and a bowl of milk.

"No, Rameses," he was saying, "if you don't drink this milk, you'll never grow horns. What will you do about wolves?"

"Are you a priest?" I demanded.

He looked at me with surprise. "A minor priest. I'm new at the temple."

"Can you drive out demons?"

"Depends. I've had more practice with animals than people. But of course the same demons get them both."

He was beardless, full- but not fat-faced, stocky but not corpulent. His hair, which was neither perfumed nor combed, climaxed his head like a bird's nest atop an oak tree. His legs were brown and hard like those of a working man. I suspected from his ease with animals that he had once been a shepherd. I liked him at once. If anyone could exorcise demons, it was such a man. His name was Zeb.

"Will you help me? My sister has been possessed."

"Of course." He touched my shoulder with sympathy, a friend comforting a friend. He dried his feet on the grass, stepped into his sandals, and returned the lamb to a pen, all with one continuous motion which belied his heavy build.

He set the vessel of milk under the lamb's nose. "Drink!" he commanded. Rameses drank.

From the temple he fetched a wicker box which I presumed to contain resinous gum, a vial of gall-water, powdered mandrake, and other simples for appeasing or repelling demons. As we hurried into the street, I described the symptoms of Rahab's possession.

He listened with close attention until I had finished. "The skin is torn, you say, and the flesh writhes. She must be fighting back. Weak people give over their bodies without a struggle. You can only see the demon by looking into their eyes, which change color and look back at you like wary little foxes."

41

"Since Rahab fought back, the demon should be easier to exorcise, shouldn't he?"

"Not necessarily. As the demon gains control, he gathers strength from his victim. A strong victim gives him all the more strength."

"What will you do then?"

He shrugged sadly. "Perhaps the taste of gall-water will drive him—or them—away."

He gasped as we entered the house. "The clay animals—you're the one who makes them! I've seen your bears in the marketplace."

I hurried him across the room. He looked wistfully over his shoulder. "And your wolves too."

"If you save her, you can take your choice."

A stranger stared at me from this familiar bed. I thought: They have taken Rahab and left another changeling.

"Bard," she whispered. "Have I died? I feel disembodied." Only the voice and the eyes, murex-purple, belonged to Rahab. The white of her skin was luminous instead of pallid. The hair, though damp against her scalp, was quicksilver tipped with blue sparks, like foam reflecting the sky. I looked at her breasts and thought of wild strawberries in a snow bank.

I must have blushed. She saw my expression and, realizing her nudity, reached for the corner of a coverlet. She paused in the motion, held her hands in front of her eyes, and she gazed at them with disbelief. She turned them in the light, bending the tiny fingers, clasping them together and staring into her palms.

"But—I am someone else."

Her hands began to explore. She touched her breasts

42

with hesitant fingertips; caressed her thighs with the wonder of discovery. I followed her movements, a discoverer myself, until I remembered that a brother does not look at his sister in such a fashion.

"Is this my soul, Bard?"

"I never saw a soul, but I don't think so."

"Touch me. We must make quite sure."

I touched her.

"Here." She guided my hand across her face. "What do you feel?" She guided my hand across her breasts. "Now?"

I felt as if I had thrust my hand into a swarm of bees. "Definitely not a soul. You're very—uh, bodily."

"And my face. What is it like?"

"Ivory." It was Zeb who spoke. I had almost forgotten him. "New ivory. Not the yellow kind."

"Hard, you mean?"

"No. White and perfect."

"But my other body. Where is that?"

Zeb looked baffled. He did not know that there had been another body. Now he saw—all three of us saw—that what had seemed to be a bundle of discarded clothes was a linen undergarment intertwined with brittle skin and hard folds of flesh.

"Like a snake," he gasped, drawing back and making the circle of Shin with his fingers. "She's shed her skin like a snake."

"No," I cried angrily. "Like a luna moth. The chrysalis is broken, and now—"

"And now I have wings." She sat up in bed and turned her back to us. Slender, translucent, opalescent, they flickered as naturally from her shoulders as flames from a hearth.

"Bard," she said, "will you bring me your mother's mirror?"

For three days Rahab refused to leave the house. She spoke little; she busied herself with trimming her old brown tunic to fit her new body. I was touched when I saw her cutting holes for her wings. Touched and terrified. My plain little sister had become a beautiful and enigmatic woman. I had to remind myself that she was only—but how old was she? I had supposed her to be of about my own age. Now, she had left me at sixteen and assumed years even as she shed ugliness. Her features held the fresh purity of dawn, but there were many mornings in her eyes.

"We must go to the market," I said. "You'll want new tunics. Colored ones. Striped ones. Trimmed ones. Rings and bracelets and—"

Her silence alarmed me. She was studying herself in a bronze mirror shaped like a partridge. She did not seem to be admiring her beauty so much as deciding its function.

"Rahab, did you hear me?"

"No, Bard, I'm afraid I didn't. I was thinking that my—metamorphosis, would you call it?—didn't come without a price. I was wondering in what currency I'll be called on to pay. Come and stand beside me. Look into the mirror. There now." Our faces were framed in the bronze. "My silver and your red. Our flames burn together at last."

"They always did."

"No. My ugliness ill became you."

"I liked you as you were."

"I was comfortable for you. I made no demands."

"Will you now?"

She laughed. "Who knows? I may spend all your silvers on gowns and trinkets."

"That's what I've just been saying. That you *ought* to buy some things."

She looked at me searchingly; as if, with a new body, she had to look at me in a new way; reexamine and reappraise.

"I do love you," she said. "You're much too serious for sixteen and you lose your temper at the drop of a head-band. But I wouldn't trade you for Shin himself."

"There's not much of me to trade."

Someone rapped on the wall beside the door. The pattern of knocks, gentle but persistent, indicated Zeb, who had been a frequent guest in the few days since Rahab's metamorphosis. He was also a welcome guest. I lifted the curtain with eagerness.

"I brought you this," he said, presenting a small wooden pail with a leather handle, and including both of us in his presentation. "Camel's milk. There's only one camel in Jericho, and this is her milk."

Rahab smiled with a witchery which was all the more bewitching because it was uncalculated and unpremeditated. I would have to caution her about her smiles. They could turn a man's head.

"We ought to be bringing *you* presents. And your god."

"Oh, no. Shin's not like Astarte. He doesn't want presents. He does things just for the doing."

"Like you," I said. "But I want you to have your pick of my animals. I don't like to sell the best ones. I like to give them a home."

"No, really," he protested. "Unless—"

"The bear?"

"Yes!"

"The wolf goes with the bear. You can't separate them. They're friends."

He took an animal in each hand. "I don't want to separate them. I have to go now. It's time to feed the camel. If I forget, she bites the chief priest. He's already talking about how much Shin would enjoy a camel steak for his next hecatomb." He paused in the door, "I *particularly* like the bear."

I could see why. There was something of a bear in his own stocky frame enclosed by its unkempt tunic, which was purple as always in honor of his god and which looked as if it had been chewed by goats. Solidity without grossness. Rusticity without ungainliness. Amiability without weakness. That was Zeb.

"You'll come back?" Rahab asked.

"Yes!"

I really must speak to her about her smile.

At the end of the week I exercised a brother's prerogative and insisted that Rahab accompany me to the market.

"Do it for me," I said. "I want people to see you."

"But what if they stare at me?"

"Look through them as if they were money lenders." My only concession was to let her hide her wings with one of my mother's cloaks.

People stared from the moment we left the house. The gatekeeper stared and strutted out of his tower with questions on his tongue.

"You have wings under your cloak, haven't you?" He was a garrulous Egyptian—all Egyptians are garrulous away from Egypt—bare-chested, loinclothed, proud of his adequate muscles and flaunting them to the fat Jerichites.

She smiled and lifted her cloak. "How did you know?"

"There was another one like you. Ten years ago. Silver Fire, we called her. No one knew where she came from but we knew where she went all right. Into a sarcophagus! She **was** throttled by one of her lovers."

Rahab frowned and walked away from him. I hurried after her through the gate.

"Just like the first one," he called to me. "Watch her, Red Top!"

The market was relatively quiet. The image-maker to whom I sold my clays had not yet appeared with his cart and baskets. The foodmongers were having no trouble disposing of eggs, geese, and butter, nor the blacksmiths of knives and clubs, but the jewelers, clothiers, and toy makers were idling in front of their stalls or talking among themselves with the worried tones of men who foresee a threat to their livelihood. News from the east bank of the Jordan was ominous. The Wanderers, it seemed, were fretting to break camp and cross the river.

"But they can't swim it at flood time," a clothier was saying. "Not all of them."

"Remember the Red Sea?"

"Yes, but that was forty years ago. Yahweh—is that their god?—hasn't produced a miracle in a long time." The clothier looked up and saw Rahab. He dipped in a chest of papyrus bark and produced a pair of red leather boots with tips of electrum.

"Antelope leather from the land of Punt. The smallest I have. You'll not get another pair to fit those dainty feet. And notice the sharp tips. You can use them for

47

prodding an ass or discouraging lechers. In your case, the second use should come in handy."

"You don't think I need a veil?"

"A veil would be a desecration."

She bought the boots. And anklets of tortoise shell. And copper bracelets. She bought a tunic of imported Egyptian linen—softer than Jerichite—dyed red with cochineal and trimmed with fox fur. She bought vials of black antimony for her eyes and carmine for her lips and perfumed olive oil for her complexion. She spent the last of my silvers.

"Metamorphosing is expensive," she said ruefully when she saw the state of my purse. "Shall I return the tunic or the boots?"

"You shall wear them for me tonight." I took her arm and we walked home in triumph. I was sorry, though, that she did not seem a little more embarrassed by all the stares. Perhaps after all she needed a veil.

When we reached the house, Zeb was waiting for us in the front room. He was sitting on a mat with a fennec curled in his lap.

"Rahab," I said. "It's the one we found in the desert! He followed me part of the way home the day you metamorphosed. But I lost him in my hurry to get you back."

"He must have seen where you lived," she said. "He's been here several times when you were in the market. I forgot to tell you."

"We don't have any at the temple," said Zeb. "Do you think he would get on well with a hyena?"

"Bard," said Rahab suddenly. "Will you go back to the market for me? I left my boots with the clothier."

The clothier did not have the boots. Perhaps Rahab

had dropped them on the way home. I carefully retraced our steps. Never mind, I would buy her another pair. It was fun to buy her clothes. She was like a child at her first harvest festival.

I met Zeb as he left the house. I saw in his face what Rahab had become. . . .

She was neither remorseful nor defiant. She had painted her lips with carmine exactly the color of her new Egyptian tunic, and her violet eyes were edged with antimony. The fennec, coiled on her pallet of palm leaves (coiled, I say, not curled—there was something serpentine about his grace) watched us without blinking.

"I asked Zeb to come," she said.

"I heard you ask him. As a friend, no more!"

She patted my hand with the maddening solicitude of a sister. "Do you think that quiet young man would have made love to me if I hadn't provoked him?"

"He used to be a shepherd. Shepherds take love where they find it."

"I did provoke him, though. His sympathy, not his lust. I told him that I was ashamed of my wings. That I felt like a freak whom no one could love."

"You're trying to say he didn't desire you?"

"Of course he desired me." It was not a boast, it was a simple assertion. "He's passionate as well as gentle. The gentlest men are always the most passionate. But it was sympathy which conquered his scruples."

"He was my friend."

"That's why he had scruples."

"Did you have to pick Zeb?"

"There was no one else I knew."

49

"And there had to be someone?" I was trying to understand the hunger which comes from years of ugliness. How the beauty which had made her desirable had also made her wish to explore desire. "You mean you were curious? You wondered what it was like to make love?"

"It wasn't curiosity at all. It was a kind of pain. A terrible absence, as if my blood were draining away and I had to staunch the flow. I thought that Zeb could ease me."

"Did he?"

"Yes. Though any man would have done." She crossed the room, and her wings rustled behind her like willow leaves in the rain. She seemed to move in music, and the music was motion as well as sound. The fennec was watching her with a chillingly human expression. I had seen such a look in the eyes of a priest who had acquired a rare alabaster image of Astarte. Perceptive; appreciative; proprietary. . . .

I went to the temple of Shin to look for Zeb. I found him removing a splinter from the foot of his hyena. The animal was standing patiently on three legs while Zeb probed and prodded with a needle.

"If you've come for a fight," he said, "we'll go into the street. Fights are forbidden in the garden. They set a bad example for the animals, who might take to eating each other." He caught the splinter with a quick swooping jab and held it up to the light. "Half a finger long! No wonder she's been limping." The hyena began to circle the garden on four triumphant legs; the other animals eyed her warily and moved out of her path.

"Rahab told me you weren't to blame," I said.

"Here," he said, pointing to the lotus pool. "Sit down." We removed our sandals and trailed our feet in the water.

"You know," he said, "I was very hesitant. Of course I desired her—what man wouldn't?—and we shepherds are noted for amorous inclinations. But—"

"You thought about me?"

"Yes, I did. I even asked her how you would feel. She said you knew about her—that she had been that way before she emerged, but now she could discriminate. That you would rather have her with me than someone else. That's why I couldn't understand when you tried to hit me as I left your house."

"You didn't hit me back. You just pushed me away and went on down the stairs. You could have broken my jaw with one tap."

"I don't like to break jaws, especially yours. I like to heal them."

"Will you make love to her again?"

"No. Not since I know how you feel. Besides, I don't really think she likes me. That way, I mean. She might have been asleep the whole time. Of course I'm out of practice now that I'm a priest. People bring me their animals but not their daughters. If I were just a priest of Astarte—! Bard, are you still angry with me?"

"No, Zeb."

He seemed unconvinced. "I'll give you back the wolf and the bear, if you like."

I felt a rush of affection for him; for anyone who could be a shepherd and a priest and a bear and a little boy at the same time. I felt very old and protective; my years were a heavy mantle on my shoulders.

51

"Of *course* you will keep the animals, and I'll make you another tomorrow. Anything but a fennec."

"You're very understanding. Sometimes I forget you're only sixteen."

We trailed our feet in the water. The lotuses lifted their lazuli chalices to catch the sun. Goldfish, like splinters of sunlight, flashed among the stems. The animals around us were hushed and docile. Even the hyena had finished its circumambulations. It was Zeb's garden, Zeb's menagerie. There was no need for Shin in such a place; Zeb was the god, and his power lay in love. He was real and solid and close, not quicksilver like Rahab. Whatever he did, he could explain and I could understand. He was my first friend.

"Things will be different soon," he said. "Better or worse."

"When the Wanderers come?"

"Yes. Two of them were seen swimming the Jordan. Naked and carrying their robes on their heads."

"Scouts?"

"Or spies."

IV

EVERYBODY knew about the spies, from King Akha in his palace of red sandstone to the one-eared butcher who sold dog meat to undiscriminating shoppers. That was the way with news in Jericho. It was told in the

52

market and retold from house to house; it spread with the rapidity and thoroughness of a sandstorm. Especially news about the Wanderers. It seemed that a shepherd had followed a stray lamb down to the banks of the Jordan. He had found his lamb in a clump of aspen trees, but the climb had been steep—the river, as you know, lies at the bottom of a steep rift—and he stopped to rest near the bank. Then he heard voices. Careful to remain concealed, he peered through the flat-stemmed, fluttering leaves and saw two young men—two young giants—climb out on the bank, shake themselves, and don the robes which they had kept on their heads while they crossed. He would have followed them (he said) but he had to get to his flock. Besides, he had seen them hide daggers under their robes, and their eyes looked gleeful and devilish, as if they would slip a blade between a man's ribs and stir him into the cooking pot. When he brought his flocks into town that night, he told his story to the gatekeeper.

Now it was the next evening, and no one knew what had happened to the two spies. The square woolen robes which they called Simlahs were like those of many desert people, and the tongue they spoke was close enough to Jerichite so that they could be understood without difficulty. They would have had no trouble entering the town. The gatekeeper did remember two young men with a pronounced accent; in fact, he had asked them their nationality. The had answered that they lived in the Canaanite city of Gezer to the west and had come to Jericho to visit a kinsman. Since Gezer, like Jericho, owed allegiance to the pharaohs, he had let them pass. Now, however, the city was alerted and the citizens were cautioned to report any strangers within the walls.

"I hope they get away," said Rahab, looking both sinful and ethereal in a tunic whose undulating cloth —silk was it called?—had been woven by worms in some unpronounceable country far to the east. The tunic was as blue as the lovely, lethal waters of the Dead Sea, and she had caught it at her waist with a scarlet sash which accented the speck of carmine I allowed her to paint on her lips. As for her wings, she had learned to emphasize their grace and fragility while minimizing their strangeness. No one could see where they joined her shoulders. They seemed inseparable from the silken folds of her gown.

She was pounding a stalk of flax with a wooden mallet to separate the fibers from the woody pulp. Other stalks lay submerged in a pot of water—they required ten days of soaking—and still others lay on the roof to bleach in tomorrow's sun. She felt that she had been a spendthrift with my silvers. To economize, she had promised to make all future tunics out of linen. Her last purchase had been a hand loom, for which she had traded six of my best animals.

"I hope they get away," she repeated. "And come back with Joshua—isn't that their leader's name? Jericho could use some manly men."

"Don't forget Zeb," I reminded her. I could not forget that she had fallen asleep in the midst of seducing him. In one way I was pleased; in another, I resented the slight to his manhood.

"You're right," she said. "Sometimes he's very helpless, though." Now she was drawing the flax fibers into thread with a wool carder's comb. "Like remembering

54

to change his tunic. Or cut his hair. You ought to remind him to visit a barber soon, or people will mistake him for his hyena."

"In the first place, he doesn't remotely resemble a hyena. A bear, possibly, but not a hyena. In the second place, he grows his hair long to make his animals feel at ease. It looks like fur to them. In the third place, if he did need to be told it's too long, why should I tell him? I'm his friend, not his barber."

"Because you have an aptitude for brothering people. First Ram. Then me. Now Zeb."

"You don't think people resent my bad disposition?"

"Oh, you get impatient at times, even cross. But it's because you love us. We know that. The remarkable thing about your brothering is that you're only sixteen."

"Only? I think that's quite mature. Almost middle-aged. The average life span for a Jerichite is thirty-three."

"That's because they overeat and make love between meals. You'll live to sixty. So you aren't middle-aged."

All this talk about brothering was not to my taste. Rahab was confirming what I had always feared, that I lacked animal magnetism because of my height. Everybody's brother and nobody's lover. I almost wished that I overate and made love between meals, even if I had to die at thirty-three.

"I suppose," I said, "that it's better to be called brotherly than fatherly."

Someone rapped on the wall. I thought of Zeb, but the raps continued beyond the point of politeness; in fact, they became peremptory. I walked to the door and lifted the curtain. Two young giants, flushed and breathless, looked at me as if I were an obstacle.

"I heard you after the first rap," I growled. "The next fifteen were superfluous."

"Could you shelter us for the night?" asked the older of the pair. I could understand him perfectly, but there was an intonation in his words, a melodiousness, which was not Jerichite. He dropped his voice in the last word of every sentence, almost like a harp of boxwood trailing into silence. "The caravanseries are full."

I started to answer, "Then sleep in the stables." But I remembered my good manners when I saw his fatigue and hunger. I also remembered that two spies were loose in the city: tall young men with accents.

"Come in," I said quickly, drawing them into the room and feeling ashamed of my petulance. "Take off your robes and make yourselves at home.

They spread the robes on the floor and sat on them, crossing their legs. Under their robes, they wore loin-cloths. They were admirably muscular without being muscle-bound, like men who have gathered their sinews through strenuous daily living. The elder—he must have been a ripe twenty-two—smiled, sighed, and relaxed. I made up my mind that I was going to dislike him. For one thing, his tallness amounted to insolence. For another, he had the kind of rawboned handsome-ness which is irresistible to all women, and his black glossy, and tumultuous hair would strike most women as preferable to woodpecker-red. I saw Rahab looking at him with appreciation. I wished a foot off his height and noticed with wicked pleasure that his feet were much too large even for his outsized frame.

The younger man—nineteen perhaps?—attended him with a worship which approached idolatry. Desert suns had bleached his hair to the sereneness of dead palm leaves. There was no real color in him anywhere, not even his eyes or his mossy eyebrows. A drab, shambling creature, I decided, in spite of his powerful build. I could trust him with Rahab (and her with him).

She had crossed the room to the cupboard to fetch some goat's milk. When she turned her back, she revealed her wings. The strangers ogled her.

"A heavenly visitant?" whispered the younger man.

"Wrong sex, but you never can tell. May be a new breed," came the reply. "Have you always lived here?" he inquired of Rahab. His teeth were free of berry stains and as white as bleached linen.

"About a year."

"Ah. And you're from distant parts?"

"I think so."

"Up or down?"

"I don't remember."

"I thought you might be what came to Abraham and told him Sara was going to bear a child at the age of ninety."

"This Sara you speak of must have been very resourceful. But what was it that came to her husband?"

"Heavenly visitants. Three of them. The male sort. Most of them are. I thought perhaps you were an exception."

"I've never seen a heavenly visitant, but I take it they carry messages from the gods. No, I'm afraid I carry nothing from the gods." She looked at me. "Except possibly misfortune."

"Well," said the elder, doubtless feeling that he had been too personal, "whatever you are, it's becoming. One last question. Where did you get *him?*"

"*Him* owns the house," I started to snort. Then I saw

that he meant our ubiquitous fennec, who unseen and unheard had entered through the curtain and ensconced himself on the oven. I resisted the urge to light a fire.

"He followed us home from the desert," she said. "Since then he's come and gone whenever he liked."

"I've seen them in the desert. I didn't know they were ever house pets."

"He thinks we're *his* pets," I said. "Look at the smug way he twitches his tail. As if he owned the house."

Rahab frowned, at whom or what I was not sure, and handed a cup of milk to the bleached young man. His name was Aram. He inspected it, tasted it, and passed it to his idol, whose name was Salmon.

"It's fresh," he said with surprise.

"In the desert we drink it rancid," Salmon explained. "Because we have to. My friend likes to wait on me out of deference to my years."

"Not only his years. His prowess. He can hit a partridge with a slingshot at a hundred yards. I've seen him fight off three wolves with one stave. And as for women—"

Salmon punched him. "Rahab isn't interested in my prowess."

"That's what you think," I muttered.

By now Rahab was passing a bowl of peppercorns. Unless you had seen her, you would hardly suppose that a woman could make an act of seduction out of passing peppercorns. They might have been dormice baked in poppy seeds, and she herself the dessert. Then she asked a surprising question:

"How many of you are there across the Jordan?"

The young men looked at her with mutual stupefaction.

She laughed. "Our city covers nearly six acres. There are fifteen hundred inhabitants. The Egyptian garrison numbers fifty men. We can muster five hundred soldiers of our own, if you count boys and old men. The walls are our best defense. Topple them or scale them and you have the city. There now. Is that what you came to learn?"

"We're from Gezer," began Aram. "We've come to—"

"Spy," finished Salmon. "You're right, Rahab, we're what you call the Wanderers. We call ourselves the Israelites, though Yahweh knows we've done our share of wandering. I suppose the whole city knows we're here. We've been chased by mongrels, fishwives, and Egyptians. All were fat. Otherwise, we would have been caught. We saw your house on the wall. The *only* clean house. We climbed the stairs hoping and here we are. Are you going to send for the guards?" There was no threat in his question, but I saw the hilt of a dagger protruding from his loincloth.

"If I meant to turn you over to the guards, I would have drugged your milk and slipped away after you fell asleep. I have no liking for the Jerichites. Their enemies are my friends."

"And you, Bard?" He looked at me with a plea which was as much for friendship as for protection. I forgot my resolve to dislike him. "I wish you would knock down the walls and ravish the women," I said. "That is, if your taste runs to girth."

"Is this a Jerichite speaking?" he laughed.

"I'm a Cretan and I live here under duress."

"Do all Cretans have red hair?"

"Only those whose ancestor was a woodpecker."

"It's nothing to be ashamed of. Most of us have an

59

eccentric or two in our family tree." Wistfulness crept into his voice. "I've never seen Crete. I've never seen the sea. Not even the Red Sea which my father and grandfather crossed with Moses. I've never seen anything but—that." He pointed toward the desert.

"Imagine a jasper set in aquamarine. That's Crete."

"I can see it," he said simply. "I can see its wonder just from seeing this room and the animals. Nobody could have modeled them who hadn't come from a wondrous country."

I fetched a skin of pomegranate wine, the prize of our cupboard, and Rahab served dried figs and bread baked with honey, which the spies ate with relish, though they quickly declined the locusts which she offered them on skewers. Salmon explained that the Wanderers had lost their appetite for locusts before they left Egypt. As for myself, I relished the juices, sweet and syrupy, which squirted from the crisp skins. Rahab had broiled them to perfection (inferior cooks wizen them).

Being implicated with spies made me feel adventurous instead of treacherous. You might expect me to owe allegiance to the town where I lived, but Jericho was neither good nor beautiful and, unlike Sodom and Gomorrah, even lacked the distinction of excessive wickedness. It made you think of a eunuch, round of belly, smiling of manner, and altogether indifferent that his king may be poisoning his own children or plotting to overrun the next country. The Wanderers and their two spies, I felt, even the bleached one, were more deserving than the entire city, except of course for Zeb, who was worth all of Canaan. I wished for him now to share the adventure and to hear Rahab sing about some

Phoenician murex fishermen. Her voice was low and clear and woundingly sweet. She did not need the accompaniment of a lyre:

> "Oh, fishers
> For the Tyrian dye,
> When queens of Sidon,
> Wearied of carmine,
> Crushed jade,
> And malachite,
> Wept for rarities,
> Did you not think
> Beauty and peril
> Inseparable
> And mock the thousand talons of the sea
> To net the purple murex?"

We sat bemused in the silent aftermath of her song. It was she who broke the silence: "I'm very tired. Will you forgive me if I leave you now?"

Much as I liked her songs, I felt a secret relief, since Salmon had been looking at her as if he had just crossed the desert and she was a palm tree. She drew some mats together to make beds for Salmon and Aram, folding their robes into pillows, and I sought my usual place on the palm leaves.

The fennec followed her from the room.

"He's keeping an eye on her," said Salmon.

"What do you mean?" I asked suspiciously.

"So she won't fly away. Is there a window in her room?"

"Yes, but her wings aren't functional."

"Moonlight doesn't need wings."

Aram fell noisily to sleep within a few minutes. His snores were clangorous.

"He dreams about conquests," Salmon explained. "He's always razing cities and carrying the women off to be his concubines. To wake him, you have to box his ears."

Talking to Salmon was easy and pleasant. He seemed a friend instead of a stranger, an equal in age and experience. I told him what I remembered of Crete. The bull games fascinated him, and he loved my description of the court ladies with their bare breasts. When I came to their painted nipples, he boxed Aram's ears.

"Aram, the Cretan ladies show their breasts. And paint their nipples!"

"What color?"

"What color, Bard?"

"Red."

"Keeps them from getting sunburned," muttered Aram, instantly asleep again to dream of concubines.

"You sleep too," I said to Salmon, resolving that Rahab's curtain would not be disturbed. "I'll wake you before it's light and lower you down the wall."

I emptied my robes and tunics on my pallet, sat in their midst like a woodpecker in its nest, and began to knot them together into a cord. I calculated as I knotted. Thirty feet of wall. The last five feet could be jumped, but I must allow a few additional feet for tying to an object in the house, the worktable perhaps, which was too large and heavy to be dragged through the window. My head began to nod . . . the cord slipped from my fingers. I recaptured it, lost it again, recaptured . . .

I awoke with the feeling that there was something I had to do. Finish the cord, that was it. But no, I had joined the last tunic before falling asleep. I looked around the room to refresh my memory. As always, I had left a lamp burning in a wall niche. Aram had not stirred. Salmon's pallet, though, was empty. Perhaps he had gone to relieve himself on or over the wall (Cretan water closets were unknown in Jericho). I thrust my head through the curtain. He was not on the wall. He must, therefore, be in Rahab's room.

I sat down on my pallet with more disgust than surprise. I already knew her inclinations, and Salmon, I suspected, could incline a temple virgin to promiscuity. I was only her brother. I was not going to burst in on her like an outraged husband. No, I was going to be sick. I felt as if a bat were using my throat for a nest. I could feel its spiny wings, its fur-rounded body.

I refused to look at him when he came from her room. I would pretend him out of the house, out of the city: drowned in the Jordan or eaten by a mountain lion.

"I woke you," he said. He was solicitous but not apologetic.

"She didn't turn into moonlight, did she? You see, she's quite earthly in some ways."

"She came for me, Bard. After you had gone to sleep."

"And snatched you into the room with her. All seven feet of you."

"Six and a half. No, I went willingly enough. Eagerly, I might say. It seemed the proper ending for the whole adventure. You're lost in a hostile town. A beautiful woman gives you shelter. Then she gives you herself. In my place, would you have refused?"

"No," I admitted. "Not if she was *very* insistent."

"Has she done this before? I rather supposed that it was habitual."

"Once before. But it's hard to get used to. It's like being locked in a dungeon, I expect. When you get out, you remember what it was like, but it's your mind that remembers, not your body. Then you're thrown back in, and you have to get used to it all over again."

"If it's any comfort, she didn't find me attractive." He sounded puzzled and rueful.

"How do you know?"

"She went to sleep." It was the ultimate confession.

"Don't you Wanderers have a commandment which says you shouldn't fornicate? I expect you haven't had much practice. It must be like wrestling. You have to learn the holds."

He smiled. "I know the holds, Bard. The way I look at it is this. There are Ten Commandments. That's a lot, isn't it, for a hot-blooded young man to obey? After all, I'm not Moses. I keep most of them. I honor my parents. I don't make graven images, not even little clay animals. But nobody can keep *every* commandment. I do fornicate when something comes my way. You might even say I do a bit of foraging."

Aram, awake at last, interjected, "In camp we call him the Stud."

"You see, it wasn't the practice I lacked. Or the wherewithal, I might add. Rahab just didn't like me. It must be my big feet." He stared dolefully at his toes. "All that walking we do. Up mountains. Over river beds. Feet get bigger and bigger."

"You know what they say," said Aram. "Big feet, big —"

Salmon was not listening. "She might have been on

64

the moon. Cool. Remote. Unreachable. And it's no wonder. Nobody wants to be kicked and stepped on by feet like battering rams. And that blasted fennec was watching the whole time."

I began to feel sorry for him. "I think your feet are exactly right for the kind of life you lead. I'm sure Rahab didn't hold them against you. The truth is, nobody seems able to please her."

"If Salmon can't, nobody can," pronounced Aram.

"She talked about you most of the time. Before she fell asleep, that is. It's a pity you're her brother."

"Actually, I'm not. Not by blood, that is—"

THUMP. THUMP. THUMP.

The blows of a fist reverberated from the next house. "Open for the King's guards!"

"Shades of Shin," I cried. "The Egyptians are searching the houses!"

"Hide them on the roof," said Rahab, standing in her door and looking neither remote nor cool, but quietly determined. "Under the flax."

I led them out of the house and pointed to the ladder. "Climb it and draw the flax down over your bodies. When the guards come out of the next house, they won't be able to see you."

When the guards came to our door—three of them, bustling like an army—I answered without haste; with in fact, the befuddlement of one who has been aroused from sleep. Rahab had returned to her room as soon as she knew that the spies were on the roof.

They were not unpleasant. Egyptians are unctuous even when they are sentencing you to be eaten by crocodiles. The leader grinned; I recognized the man who often served at the gate, the one who liked to display his adequate brawn.

He remembered me at once. "If it isn't Red Top! This must be the house of our latest Silver Fire."

"If you mean Rahab, yes."

"Where is the—er—lady?"

"Asleep."

"Alone?"

"Except for a fennec, yes."

"Seen any spies tonight?"

"No."

"The lady seen any?"

"Rahab," I mumbled through her door. "Have you seen any spies?"

"What's this talk about spies?" She blinked, scintillating into the room with tousled splendor. "You mean they're still at large?"

He paused to relish her touslement. "If they're in the city, that is. Personally, I don't think they ever got by the gate. You know those two men who said they were from Gezer? I think they really were. I don't think they were spies at all. No one who wasn't from Gezer would say he was. Ever see the place? More pigs than people."

"You may be right," I said. "Those Wanderers are brave enough in the desert, but here with you Egyptians —well, that's an ass of a different color."

He chuckled over the platitude, which was as old as the pyramids. "I wish I had thought of that. Ass of a different color. Heh! Well, if you see any spies, send for me." He added, exclusively to Rahab, "If you don't, send for me anyway." Convulsed at his own roguery, he clapped his silent friends on the shoulder and shoved them toward the next house.

"Open up for the King's guards!"

Aram was stifling a sneeze when he climbed down the ladder—the flax had tickled his nose—but otherwise the two spies seemed none the worse for their concealment. It was time for their departure. Dawn must find them far from the city.

Salmon gave me his robe as a parting gift. I started to refuse. I knew that a Simlah was a Wanderer's most precious possession.

"It'll weigh me down," he explained. "Besides, you can use it for a blanket."

We gathered in Rahab's room beside the window which overlooked the walls. Aram estimated the distance to the ground and nodded approval at the length of my cord. He tied the end to a leg of the worktable and wedged the table in the doorway between the rooms.

"I'll go first," he announced. "Enjoyed the pomegranate wine. Don't get that in the Wilderness, you know. Manna's nourishing but not too tasty."

Salmon was exchanging farewells with Rahab. He caught her hand and squeezed the fingers. It was probably the chastest farewell he had ever exchanged.

"Rahab," he said earnestly. "You were wearing a scarlet sash tonight. Before we come again—all of us this time, Joshua and the whole tribe—you must hang it over the curtain in your front door. It will be a sign that you and Bard sheltered us. Whatever happens, you must stay in the house until I come for you."

"I have a friend named Zeb," I said. "If he's in the house, will he be spared too?"

"Not Egyptian, I hope. No chance for them."

67

"Jerichite, but not like the rest. A priest."

"Sacrifice babies?"

"No. Not even lambs. Used to be a shepherd."

"Shepherds are all right."

We watched them race down the mound and veer to the west of the city, away from the gate and the Moon Spring and the early farmers who beat the dawn to the fields. . . .

She knelt beside my pallet and spread Salmon's Simlay over my arms and chest. "Good night, brother."

"It's almost morning."

"Go to sleep quickly."

"Will you sing to me? Like you did to the spies."

"One song then.

> "The tide, withdrawing,
> Scatters a ruinous opulence:
> Sea-wrack and the purple murex,
> Coral whose sharp and roseate fingers
> Fumble a pirate's plunder.
>
> Beloved, go,
> Obedient to the moon's compulsion.
> I am not indigent
> Who have the sea-gold of your passing,
> Nor shall I much protest
> If coral fingers bruise the sand."

"But that's too sad."

"All true songs are sad."

"Where did you learn it?"

"I made it up just now." She kissed me on the cheek.

"Rahab. Will there be others like Salmon?"

"No."

"I'm happy then."

"Happiness is for gods and fools "

V

I AWOKE with the feeling that today I would model such an image that the king himself would hold it in his hands and say: "No real animal ever looked like this. It is much too beautiful." Today I would walk in the market with Rahab and the merchants would smile without wanting my silvers, and the dogs would have glossy fur instead of mange, and the pigs would not be odorous. The Egyptian guards would talk excitedly about the spies— Who had seen them, sheltered them, helped them to escape?—and Rahab and I would nod to each other and smile with secret knowledge.

I splashed water on my face from a pitcher and peered at myself in a mirror to see if I needed to shave. Alas, not yet. Perhaps next week? Astarte curse those bronze mirrors! Their reflections were never clear. For all I knew, there might be a presentiment of whiskers on my chin. I sprinkled my hair with olive oil, combed it with a tortoise shell comb, and anchored it with a fillet. Even in the dim bronze, it looked distressingly red, but this morning I refused to be distressed.

I stepped into one of the tunics—this one was green

and caught at the waist with a crimson belt—which had recently served as a part of the cord for the spies. I did not begrudge a few wrinkles, a streak of dirt, for so worthy a cause.

"Rahab," I called. "Get up! The cocks crowed an hour ago. I'll go to the Fountain House with you." Today I would even share her woman's work.

When she failed to answer, I lifted the curtain in her door. A carefully folded blanket reposed, fennec-like, at the foot of her pallet. A single tunic of hyacinth hung from a peg on the far wall. On her cedar chest, vials of carmine and antimony, a mirror, an unguent jar of obsidian, lay in methodical rows. I told myself that she had dressed, tidied the room, and gone to the well, though such tidiness was much more characteristic of my mother than Rahab, who was prone to scatter her tunics like so many discarded chrysalises.

The Fountain House, an Egyptian innovation, was a cool cellar hollowed out of the ground, its roof on a level with the street. Draw basins, waterproofed with hard, fine stucco, ran along three sides. Spouts in the shape of lion heads filled the basins from the Moon Stream which, as I have said, ran under the city and flowed to the surface beyond the walls. Women were dipping urns into the basin or holding them directly under the spouts.

"Rahab!"

She was not in the room. The women looked at me with amused tolerance.

"Have you seen a girl with wings?"

"She's left you already?" asked a woman whose red eyes were almost engulfed by ridges of fat, like beets in a furrow. "Never trust a girl with wings, my boy.

70

Whether she can fly or not, she still likes to travel. Besides, you can do better. A little fellow like you needs an *ample* woman, not a doll. One who'll feed you and make you grow."

"Amplitude is fine for pigs," I retorted.

"Look for her in the nearest brothel," Red Eyes squealed after me.

I would look for her, but not in a brothel, or even in the town. I knew with the knowledge which needs no confirmation that she had returned to her people. The fennec had come to guide her. She who had been to me as the wind which shakes the temple bells had left them without music, without motion. But even the wind leaves evidence of its going, a bent leaf, a bowed blade of grass.

It was time to call on Zeb.

He was sitting on a bench under a trellis clustered with grapevines. The grapevines were hard, small, and green, but somehow one saw them as they would become in the fall, purple with juice and reverberant with bees. He was holding a newborn lamb in his arms and looking like a vegetation spirit, born of the earth and bearing a part of the earth, its growth and its continuity. Creator, nurturer, comforter. To whom else should I turn?

"Bard," he cried, displaying the lamb as if it were his own son. "He was born last night. Isn't he splendid?"

"Rahab has gone."

"Where?" He looked less surprised than I expected.

"I don't know. Where she came from, I guess."

"Are you sure you want to find her?" The question struck me as impertinent, if not cruel.

"Why shouldn't I?"

71

"Because her people may harm you. She knew that, else why has she gone away without any trace?" He stood before me in his rumpled tunic, a stocky, grave-eyed young man who was also a priest, and who had never ceased to be a shepherd, and whom I loved next to Rahab. Everything he said seemed to hurt me or anger me. Everything he said strengthened my resolve to find Rahab. And yet he was probably right, and he spoke from concern, not carelessness.

"She's gone away because they called her. But I can call her too—in the other direction. But first I have to find her. And my brother Ram. They ought to be in the same place. Can you help me, Zeb?"

"Track her, you mean?" He thought for a moment. "I haven't any dogs—I won't keep these Jerichite mongrels. They would harry my sheep. You've seen the hyena, though. Her sense of smell is keener than a dog's."

"But hyenas rob graves and steal babies!"

"Not if you feed them properly," he said, aggrieved. "They're very much misunderstood. Loyal, affectionate, and obedient."

"Has yours been properly fed?"

"She's just finished a partridge."

"Let's get her then."

Hatshepsut resembled an oversized dog with stripes and enlarged forefeet. There was something appealing about her yellow eyes, though her grin was enigmatic. You felt that she behaved or misbehaved according to whim, and that her whims accorded to the dictates of her stomach. Zeb patted the long hair on her head.

"Notice the teeth. They can crush a partridge with one chomp." His affection for animals did not extend to birds—except woodpeckers. "She's very proud of them."

"I see she is."

"Now we must make our plans. Either Rahab went *across* the desert or *under* the desert. That is, if you're sure she didn't fly."

"Positive. Her wings can break a fall but not lift her off the ground. She jumped off my roof once to test them."

"Good. If she'd flown, we would need a griffin to track her. It's across or under then. Either way, we'll have to have provisions. I suggest a skin of water—it won't spoil like milk, and it won't dull our brains like wine. Some dates and goat's cheese for us and a slab of beef for Hat. The beef is very important. Otherwise, we can't depend on her."

"You mean she gets ravening."

"Whimsical, I would say."

His house stood in the rear of the garden, a rectangle of red plastered mud whose thatched roof came to a point and fell shaggily to left and right, like an Egyptian lady's coiffure. An edge of the roof extended to make a porch supported by two wooden posts, which Zeb had decorated none too artistically with red splashes of paint. Opening onto the porch was a single room with a couch, a chest of papyrus wood, and a cupboard. The bear and wolf I had given him looked at home on the chest, and a live cat slept on the cupboard, its plump yellow tail guarding the shelves. He lifted the tail without waking the cat and found the necessary provisions, which he packed in a leather pouch and flung over his shoulder.

"And a lamp," he said. "We'll need it if we go underground. We can keep it burning in a case of dried bladder. I have one I use for night calls."

"I wish I had known you a year ago, Zeb. Then we could have followed Ram."

"I hadn't come to Jericho yet. I was still a shepherd in the hills to the west. Never mind. We'll find him now."

"But a year's a long time for a little boy. Who's been looking after him?"

"I suspect Rahab is now."

When we entered the street with our hyena, you would have thought that we were marauding Wanderers. She trotted decorously between us, neither snapping her jaws nor howling her characteristic howl, but children pelted her with olive pits and mothers breasted their babies with indignant cries of "Beast!" and "Grave-robber!" and "Cannibal!"

"What are they talking about?" muttered Zeb. "It would only be cannibalism if she ate hyena babies."

A fish wife without a baby to risk decided to heckle us. "That a dog you fellows have there?"

"Of sorts."

"Where'd she get them stripes?"

"Painted," I snapped. "Didn't want her to look naked."

"Some dog. Why don't she close her mouth?"

Zeb stopped in his tracks. "Madam," he said, "my dog, as you call her, excels you in both cleanliness and civility. She also has better grammar. Mind your manners or she may forget hers.

"It's good she's just fed," he added to me. "She dislikes persiflage."

Once in my house, Hat immediately caught the scent from Rahab's pallet. We had to restrain her while we completed our plans.

"I suspect," said Zeb, "that the trail will lead out into the desert and then under the ground. The whole area is honeycombed with tunnels. Some are big enough for a man to crawl through."

"How far do they go?"

"Never followed one."

"Afraid of snakes?"

"Afraid of whatever built those tunnels. It doesn't want to be visited."

Hatshepsut did not lead us into the desert, however. She led us to the ruins of an old villa, a survival from the Hyksos occupation of two centuries ago. It was the one unoccupied building in the overcrowded town. Houses jostled its grounds, but the ruin itself was avoided because it was known to be the haunt of vipers and probably also of lingering Hyksos demons. Beggars hesitated to sleep beneath its partially collapsed roof and builders refused to clear the ground for newer buildings.

We groped among shadows and tumbled bricks. Where the sun penetrated through holes in the roof, the bricks were bare; in the sunless crannies, moisture had collected and lichens grew; lizards distended their orange throats and vipers reared their diminutive, deadly heads. Hat was unalarmed by the vipers and incurious of the lizards. She did not forget her quest; she did not deviate from the scent; she led us directly to a stone slab which seemed to be rooted in the floor. A frieze decorated its face with hunters spearing water birds in a papyrus swamp.

Zeb fell to his knees and ran his fingers over the slightly raised figures; paused; pressed. The stone turned on a hidden axis.

"Just as I thought. It's a trapdoor. I've heard the Egyptians build them the same way."

In the light of our lamp, we could see a staircase and two sets of prints winding into the earth: a woman's sandals and beside them the delicate paw marks of a fennec.

"She closed the slab behind her," I said sorrowfully. "And she didn't leave us a clue."

Zeb touched my shoulder. "Of course not. She didn't want you to endanger yourself. She's returning to her people, but you're an invader."

"Then so are you. More than I am. It's all very well for me to go plunging into the earth after my family. No one would miss me if I never came back. But you're different—a priest and a healer. Your animals depend on you, to say nothing of your god. Lend me Hat and go back to the temple."

"You don't know her eating habits."

My next question took me by surprise. I can only say that it was not premeditated. "Do you love Rahab?"

His answer was prompt. "I don't understand her well enough to love her. She's like a bird. She interests me. But who can tell what a bird is thinking about? And I don't mean any reflection on your ancestry, Bard. With a sheep, I know. Bland thoughts. Even with a camel. Mean thoughts, usually. Not with a bird. Not with Rahab."

"Why are you coming then?"

"Because," he said with a rare hint of impatience, "you're my friend, and you're only sixteen even if you try to act thirty, and you're going down there with vipers and fennecs and Shin knows what else, and you'll get bitten unless I come too. Now, you see, we can bite *them*. Hat will be our teeth."

76

"When we get back, I'm going to make an offering to Shin. What do you think he would like?"

"Our getting back."

At the foot of the stairs we found a tunnel whose builders were obviously different from those who had built the house. It looked as if the stairs had once led to a family burial crypt. Long after the crypt had been filled with earth, someone—something—had dug the tunnel to connect with the stairs, the trapdoor, and the town. It was just tall enough for an upright hyena or a man on his hands and knees.

"The Wanderers talk about Sheol," I said. "It's a prison for wicked souls under the earth. Do you think that's where we're going?"

"Looks more like a prison for good souls. The wicked ones are the jailers."

PART   II:

The Peoples of the Sea

VI

HAT WENT first, disposing of vipers with her powerful jaws; then Zeb, pushing our lamp ahead of him; then myself, ignobly but not unhappily bringing up the rear. At the start of our journey, the walls oozed with moisture; except for our generally horizontal direction, we felt as if we were descending into a clammy-walled well. Sometimes the oozing became an actual trickle and our knees as well as our shoulders chilled to the damp and cold. You never knew when your hand was going to grasp slime instead of clay.

"It's the Moon Stream," said Zeb. "We must be running parallel to it—probably just a few feet away. It's dampened the earth around it."

The tunnel dipped sharply and the roof raked our backs with stone talons.

"Keep talking," I said. "I feel like a bat in the sunshine."

"Those were the foundations of the walls. We've left the city. The desert lies above us. Shin only knows what lies ahead of us. No, he's the wrong god here. The moon can't see into the Underworld."

"We'll have to trust ourselves to another moon," I said. "Rahab."

"May she light us well," he said without conviction. Always, there was darkness, there was uncertainty, there was danger of vipers. But the journey proved more discomforting than dangerous, and I for one thought more about aching muscles than possible snake bites. For once I benefited from my small frame; there was less of me to insinuate through the tunnel than there was of Hat and Zeb.

After we left the city and the dampness, we found that the walls had been diligently smoothed, the dirt floor had been packed and hardened with deliberate care. Occasional chambers opened above our heads to allow us to stand and stretch; to eat cheese, drink water, and feed raw beef to a patient if nervous hyena. Then, again, the tunnel, the torturous, tortuous crawl, the apprehension and the expectation.

Our emergence was abrupt and breathtaking. We seemed to have entered the crater of a volcano. But no, it was the enclosed hollow of a mountain, for the roof arched roundly if jaggedly above us and shut us into a world of blue-silver phosphorescence like the early dusk when night is an intimation rather than a presence. I supposed from our direction and the distance we seemed to have come that we were inside of Jebel Kuruntul, the mountain which crouched behind Jericho in the shape of a lion. The Cat, it is sometimes called. Against the sky of the dome, lights flickered like stars, caves no doubt, opening to the surface.

There was, of course, a town. There had to be a town to occupy such a world; Rahab's world. In the silver-and-dusk, you might have mistaken it at first for a forest of mushrooms the size of houses. But the mushrooms were the houses. Cones or domes or cylinders; half-domes or disks atop columns; all of them, whether black, gray, orange, or white, possessing the smooth, fleshy texture of their miniature counterparts on the floor of a forest. So naturally did they rise from the white tufa rock of the earth that they seemed to have been grown instead of built. Around them, among them, like a spider web fallen to the ground, ran a concourse of streams twinkling with blue and silver sparks. It was as if the city were in thrall to the web and its unseen weavers; as if its airy caps and cones existed by sufferance. It was such a town as Rahab's people should have built; earthily ethereal and a little sinister.

Behind the town, an extraordinary column of gases—black, ocher, and umber; torrid transparencies—swirled from the ground like a waterspout and dissipated itself in the sharpness of the cavern roof. Unlike a waterspout, it remained relatively fixed; it swayed above its base but did not lash through the town so vulnerable at its foot. It was our first glimpse of the Wind Well. Happily, we did not guess its purpose.

Zeb and I stretched and gulped the cold air, which was faintly scented with musk. Hat shook the dirt from her shoulders and bared her teeth in a grin.

"It can't be described," I said. "It's beyond words."

I had spoken the obvious. I had desecrated the silence. Zeb was more respectful. Having lived with animals, he had a gift for silences. He was rapt by the scene and quite oblivious of me.

I tugged on the sleeve of his tunic. "Zeb, don't shut me out. I can't enter your thoughts."

He looked at me with astonishment. "But I was thinking *with* you."

"I'd rather you talked to me."

He laid an arm over my shoulder. "Sometimes I

don't have any words. That doesn't mean I've forgotten you."

"That's all right," I said. His rough arm was more eloquent than words. "But what *were* you thinking when you were so still?"

"What a perfect home this would make for burrowing animals. Foxes. Lizards. Mice. Men could never find them down here."

"Here come some of the inhabitants now. They seem to be people, though. And they aren't dressed for burrowing."

Two young women were approaching us with deliberate and unhurried steps. They had crossed a bridge over one of the streams and were now climbing the rise to the mouth of our tunnel. They were winged like Rahab; small of limb; delicate of feature. One who had never seen Rahab would have thought them beautiful, except that they wore blandness as a bride may wear a veil, and perhaps for the same reason: to conceal unflattering thoughts. From a distance they seemed indistinguishable. They even walked in unison, like the Egyptian guards who marched around Jericho to avoid the obesity of the natives. Their saffron tunics, caught at their waists by white sashes, fell modestly to their calves. Tiny electrum bells, shaped like moths, fluttered and tinkled at their ankles.

They smiled identical smiles. I almost expected them to have identical names. But one of them said: "I am Aspen. My friend is Olive. You were long in the tunnel. At first we thought your beast had led you astray. You are awaited in the town."

"Is Rahab here?"

"Where else? Though here we call her Moondust."

"And Ram, my brother?"

They stared at me as if I had asked for snowflakes in Egypt.

"A little boy with red hair like mine."

"Ah, Red Hair. That one is here too."

"When may I see them?"

"When you have bathed. You are quite unpresentable as you are. Black as a Libyan. And as for your beast—" Her nostrils, if not her eyes, betrayed disgust.

"Hyenas don't bathe," interjected Zeb. "It gives them the croup."

"Everyone bathes in Honey Heart." Like her companion, she carried a dagger under her sash. Its ivory hilt was figured with delicate carvings and adapted to her small fingers, but its copper blade looked very sharp.

We passed through a field of plants like griffin eggs, round, gray, tall as a child of twelve, and I recognized a gargantuan variety of the puff balls which grow in Cretan forests. Corpulent young girls with pallid features were cutting or cultivating them. One of the girls had severed a ball from its network of roots and sliced it into a dozen or more sections, which she was stacking like wood in a two-wheeled wagon drawn by foxes. The foxes, of which there were four, were fretting under their harness, and a second girl was trying to quiet them with a slice of the ball.

"They'd rather have birds," Zeb called to her.

The foxes ceased to fret. The girl smiled as if young men rarely spoke to her. "Would they?"

"And foxes shouldn't be harnessed."

"Shouldn't they?"

"No, they shouldn't. Nothing should, as a matter of fact, but if you have to harness, harness an ass."

"We don't have those here," she said, losing her smile and looking so ugly that you wanted to buy her a veil. "The Masters say that asses are uncouth."

Before Zeb could reply that couthness lay in the eye of the beholder—to him, asses looked better than most people—Aspen prodded us toward the town. "I've already said that you are *awaited*."

"But where are the fennecs?" I wanted to know. "We've only seen foxes."

"In their Dens," came the tart reply. "You wouldn't expect to find them in the fields, would you? Besides, it's their Hour of Ease."

"I would expect them anywhere. They seem to get about."

"And where are the boys and men?" asked Zeb. "Do the women do all the work?"

You would have thought from Aspen's expression that we had taken the name of Astarte in vain. "Males," she said, "neither please the eye nor tease the ear. In Honey Heart, we have learned to do without them."

Olive, speaking for the first time and reminding us that the two women were not after all indistinguishable, sighed: "Learned? Been taught, you mean."

Aspen ignored the sigh. "You two may consider yourselves honored to be received as guests. See that you comport yourselves with fitting decorum."

"I feel about as decorous as a dung-cake," Zeb whispered to me. "How about you?"

"I feel like finding Rahab before we're done without."

The town was separated from the fields by a low wall of blue glazed bricks entwined with morning glories. There was no gate; inside the wall, fox-drawn chariots glided along the streets with the muffled liquidity of boats on a lake. Their wheels were sewn in velvet, and the streets themselves were a kind of velvety grass which showed neither wheel marks nor footprints. Most of the chariots were driven by women with wings like Rahab and our own escort—Wingers they were called—but one driver was a wingless girl of perhaps ten who looked distinctly human and who slowed her team to study us as we passed.

Aspen saw my puzzlement. "She's one of the Changies. Like your brother."

Our first view of the town was brief and limited. Our destination was a house on the side facing the field of puff balls. We crossed a narrow bridge, cunningly contrived to resemble a fallen tree, and walked down an avenue where mushrooms like pollarded elms, tall, slender, round-capped, made feeble shadows in the almost-dusk.

A Winger, clad in a yellow leather tunic which appeared to be a uniform, was patrolling the grounds with a fox on a leash. She greeted our escort with some asperity.

"You were slow enough getting them here, Aspen. No matter. The Master is still in repose. You're to leave our visitors on the third level." The snout and shoulders of the fox were encased in a leather guard which matched the color of his mistress' tunic. He walked smartly; pranced I should say. He left no doubt that he knew his duties and liked to be watched performing them.

At close range the shape of the house preserved its resemblance to a mushroom, but the texture of the walls revealed itself to be tufa rock so white and weightless that you expected it to run like foam and dissolve at your feet. A circular staircase twisted around the stem and disappeared in the cap. We began to climb. The stairs, which were flat red stones projecting from the stem, looked hardly more substantial than clay shingles, and I hurried to test them ahead of Zeb. They held; in fact, they held without bending or shaking or otherwise acknowledging my passage. I was still concerned about Zeb, however.

"Keep one foot on the ground," I cautioned, "and ease your weight onto the other foot."

"Those stairs will hold a monoceros," Aspen said with, I fear, an implied aspersion on Zeb's solidity. But the stairs were too narrow for exchanging aspersions. I concentrated on keeping my balance and glancing through the oval windows as we moved from one level to the next: a kitchen where Uglies were broiling birds on spits and wrapping them in slices of puff ball; a parlor where Changies were carding wool; and then the extraordinary room where we stopped our climb. If it was to be our prison, its nature was well concealed. We seemed to have stepped into a forest dell. For a floor, there was soft green moss. For furniture, there was a tiny hillock which brimmed with jonquils and looked as if it were meant for wanderers, whether animal or human.

"Flowers growing indoors!" I cried.

Zeb was more perceptive and less appreciative. "They're artificial."

"Of course," said Aspen. "Real flowers wilt, real grass has to be cut. The growths you see here are woven from silk or cut from velvet and other materials. That's velvet under your feet, not moss. Those jonquils you see are pure silk on stems of a material we call rubber—you don't have it yet in the Sun World."

Other artifices were more apparent but no less effective. A metal brazier shaped like a fennec, even to the leaf-thin ears, warmed the air, and a flight of wind bees, chiseled from resin and suspended by invisible threads, emitted sweet tinklings and musky scents.

"Only the stream is real. We couldn't improve on the original." She pointed to a stream which flowed out of a papyrus thicket and into a rock-lined basin. "We diverted it from the ground. But I don't need to explain hydraulics to a Cretan. You have flowing water in your palaces, I believe. Or had."

She motioned us to the hillock. "It's for sitting or reclining. You won't crush the flowers. In Honey Heart, you will find that art usually surpasses nature." She began to sound as if she were reading from a papyrus scroll. "Nature has flaws. It is sometimes untidy and always undependable. Art, however, can be perfect because the artist, though himself subject to imperfections, is capable of creating ideals instead of imitations."

I was not in a mood for pedagogy. "Where is Rahab? Where is my brother?"

"Your impatience is as unbecoming as your filth. As the Masters teach, 'Patience and power dwell in the same Den.' Rest now."

Once they had gone, we investigated the hillock and found that, at least for once, art had indeed surpassed nature. The flowers invited our bodies like opiates and unguents, cushions and coverlets, all at the same time; soothed our weariness and touched sleep to our temples. Yellow flowers, green leaves. Petal-softness, leaf-silkiness.

Myrrh . . . raindrops . . . rock roses . . . Rahab . . . Raha . . . b . . .

Zeb gripped my hand. "Don't sleep, Bard. It's too perfect. It's *un*natural. There's trouble afoot, and it has big feet."

"I know. Let's sleep on it."

"Everything here is unnatural. Too big. Too small. Reversed. Whoever heard of foxes pulling chariots or mushrooms as big as monoceroses?"

"Rahab will have to explain things to us."

"Look at them, holding hands!" Two young Wingers had just entered the room. Their sandals were quite soundless on the moss. "Remember what a time our ancestors had in Sodom?" And then to me: "And where are *your* ancestors from, dear?"

"Crete. My great-grandfather wrestled a bull in the afternoon and pleasured thirteen women that night. My great-grandmother was the first."

The young women nodded approval. The more talkative of the two was as glittering as a tiger moth, even to the black and yellow stripes on her wings. "Wish we had tried Crete for our last profiting. I'm Manna, this is Luna. The Masters sent us to Ai, though. Can't say much for *that* town. Five pigs for every man, which reminds me we've come to bathe you. First we must have your clothes. You see we've brought you a change." She laid hold of my tunic.

"We can undress ourselves," I said testily.

"Hush," whispered Zeb. "We don't want to seem ungrateful, do we? There's time when submission is the better part of valor."

"*And* bathe ourselves," I said. "At least I can. My friend must speak for himself."

"Speaking for myself, I'm still tired from the tunnel. I could use some help."

"So could you," said Manna. "Besides the dirt you picked up in the tunnel, you have red clay under your fingernails. That won't do here."

"It's because of my work. I'm an artist."

"All the more reason to keep your person spotless. Uncleanliness is the delight of demons." She knelt and busied herself with removing my sandals. The leather thongs divided between her deft fingers. "There. You won't need that. Or that." She drew me to my feet and with an almost instantaneous flick undid the knot in my sash. "Now face me. Bend over. Wriggle. Ah." She held my tunic in her hands like a fisherman who has caught a prize octopus.

I was left in my loincloth, a brief tendril of linen which clothed no more than the name suggests, and Zeb was happily, helpfully undergoing a similar diminishment.

"You're *not* black all over," Manna continued, "you're a nice ruddy color to go with your hair. For a little fellow, you're well put together too. I've heard Cretans have the smallest waists in the world. I can believe it." She tried to encircle my waist with her fingers. "Not quite. Now you try mine."

"And look at this one," said Luna, pinching Zeb's arm as though she were about to purchase him in the slave market. "Sheer muscle!"

"Too much hair," complained Manna. "Head. Arms. Chest. Must be a farmer."

"Shepherd," he corrected. "Used to be anyway."

"I expect he needed all that hair to keep him warm in the fields at night," Luna defended. "That is, when he

91

didn't have a shepherdess to keep him warm! Is that right, shepherd?"

"Right."

Meanwhile, Manna was reaching for the frog-headed pin which sustained my loincloth. "There now. Into the pool with you."

The water was heated; the floor of the pool was covered with white sand. I subsided in the thigh-deep water like a netted dolphin returning to the sea.

"Shall I scrub your back?" It was Zeb, splashing stormily beside me in whatever water he had not displaced by his abrupt immersion.

"No, no," chided Manna. "That's my job. I'm trained for it, don't you know. We take lessons in such things before we go out."

"Go out?"

"Out into the Sun World to profit. Luna and I have been out twice. Ai was our second trip. Rahab has just come in from her first. But conversation must wait on cleanliness. Move over."

Luna and Manna kicked off their sandals, oscillated out of their tunics, and joined us in the water.

"Stand under the waterfall. Turn around." They began to rub us with alkaline salt and olive oil. Manna's cool hands eased over my body; the dirt oozed from my limbs. Zeb had begun to sing a little song from his shepherd days:

"Brownest, broadest, hugest, hairiest—
Of all the bears, he is beariest. . . ."

"You've wet your undergarments," he said thoughtfully, breaking off his song. "Oughtn't you to remove them?"

"Remove themselves, you mean!" The speaker was Rahab; the speech was more than a command, it was a commandment.

VII

HER WINGS gave angry flutters; her eyes implied an indiscriminate rebuke for bath, bathers, and bathed.

She arrested Manna's hand in mid-journey down my spine. "Get out, Manna. You too, Luna. I'll finish their bath."

Manna tittered, "But, Moondust, you're selfish. We don't want to waste them, do we? You know the old saying, 'Gather ye coconuts while ye may.' "

"Why don't we divide them?" suggested Luna. "The little one is yours, we know that. But can't Manna and I have the hairy one? We want to *tousle* him." Zeb beamed at the compliment.

"Out!"

"Greedy!" they called over their shoulders.

Floundering out of the pool, I forgot my nakedness, my wetness, and my oiliness, and embraced Rahab, I fear, with more than brotherly ardor.

"I can't even hold onto you!" she laughed as her hands oozed alkaline salts and olive oil. "Back into the pool with you and I'll finish your bath. And, Zeb, you don't need to clutch your tunic like a temple virgin. You forget I've seen you before!" She hugged him v.ith such enthusiasm that I felt a twinge of the old jealousy and clambered out of the pool for the second time. I was glad that he managed to retain the tunic even while he returned the hug. "Did your sheep give birth?" That was better; that was friendly, sisterly, anything but ardent. Onetime lovers who wish to rekindle passion do not talk about sheep (goats, perhaps, not sheep).

"Nine pounds!"

She caught each of us by a hand. "And you followed me here, you two. You missed me that much!" Her face grew solemn. "But you shouldn't have, you know." She forced an air of humorous chastisement. "It's good I came when I did. Manna and Luna have just recently come in from Ai. They remember their profiting rather too pleasantly."

"Weren't they supposed to give us a bath? They seemed to think that we were awfully dirty."

"They were supposed to bring you oil and fresh tunics. No one told them to stay and help. And I didn't notice much resistance from you!" She handed me a tunic, dusk-blue, with sleeves trimmed in silver.

I did not feel like playful parrying. There were too many mysteries. "Why did you leave me, Rahab?"

"Because I was recalled."

"Your people sent for you? They sent the fennec after you?"

"The fennec came for me, it's true. But he wasn't sent. Surely you've guessed by now that my people don't rule in Honey Heart. They serve the fennecs."

"The *fennecs?* Those sawed-off foxes with oversized ears?"

"I'm not surprised," said Zeb. "I can usually feel emanations from animals. But the fennec that came to your house—there was always something guarded about him."

"Quite simply, we're their slaves. We grow their food, cook for them, spin for them, spy for them, speak for them when they have to communicate with humans. They educate us, teach us to sing and play the lyre, fill our minds with apothegms about the nature of art and beauty which they expect us to spout at the clap of a paw. They build their own houses and dig their own tunnels—their claws can dig through solid rock, and there are seven towns like this one under the desert. But for other tasks, they need our hands."

Rahab looked very small and somehow breakable. What had the woman in the Fountain House called her? A doll. A terra cotta toy beloved by children, I thought, and sometimes broken by a careless hand. She drew her shoulders forward as if she were trying to warm herself with her wings. I put my arm around her. She was very cold.

"Before there were historians to record history on papyrus scrolls or stone tablets, my people lived in the desert. We could fly then. We were called the Peoples of the Sea because we frolicked above the desert like flying fish above the Great Green Sea. Peoples, not People. As you know we aren't born with wings. Our Littlies, our Uglies, and our Wingers were taken by the desert people for three separate races living together as aphids live with ants. We lived in a valley cradled by the mountains and protected from storms and bandits. High Heart, we called it. We grew comfortable, we grew complacent. We flew less often because it was pleasant to lie in our tents, which were colored like the coils of a conch shell, and tell stories about our ancestors who had fought against griffins and phoenixes among the clouds. The power of flight began to desert us. More and more of us emerged from the chrysalis with puny wings; wings incapable of lifting us over the mountains, or even off the ground. No matter, we thought. Why did we need to fly? We had our valley, we had our girdling mountains.

"Then the fennecs came. Shy little animals looking for a home. Sniffing about our tents. Standing on their hind legs and barking for food. They brought us honey combs from places to which we could no longer fly. They carried us water when our wings failed over the desert. They performed tricks for us and everyone said, 'How clever! How endearing!' Our children made pets of them.

"After a few years, they outnumbered us. And captured us. And led us into a mountain as their slaves."

"Couldn't you fight them?" I exclaimed. "One kick would break their backs."

"Yes," said Zeb. "It's not as if they were bears."

"In the temple of Astarte, you've seen the priestesses fall into a trance? The Divine Slumber, it's called. The priest has spoken an incantation over them. The fennecs exercise a similar power over us. Except it comes from their thoughts instead of their words. Without speaking, they can actually reach into our minds and implant ideas, knowledge, commands. Of course they have a language among themselves. The barks you hear represent a vocabulary of at least ten thousand words. But with us, they have to communicate by thought. Our ears are not sharp enough to follow their sounds, though they can understand every word we say. There are nearly a thousand Peoples of the Sea in Honey Heart. All of them—all of us—serve all of the fennecs. But each of us is controlled by one particular fennec whom she calls her Master and who calls her his Servitor. My own Master is Chackal, whom you met in Jericho, and this house is his Den."

"How do you serve him?" It was not a question I wanted answered; still, it had to be asked.

"If Chackal wants to command an Ugly or a Winger, he communicates through me. He thinks his command and I speak it to Luna, Manna, or whomever else he wishes to serve him. In a word, I am his intermediary with my people. He claimed me when I was a little girl and began the slow process of developing rapport. It is only Chackal who can enter my thoughts.

"Aside from passing along his commands, however, I do nothing. I am one of the Comelies, those whom the fennecs proclaim to be perfect in beauty. Decorative rather than useful. I am not allowed to spin for fear I will mar my hands. I am not allowed to walk in the fields, much less plant or harvest. I am not allowed to guard or build or paint. I sing, dance, beguile. I decorate. That is my whole existence. Fennecs are the most fastidious and sensitive of all creatures. They abhor squalor and ugliness. They could have enslaved Egyptians or Canaanites or Hittites. They chose the Peoples of the Sea because of our grace and delicacy. They found us aesthetically pleasing. They collected us as if we were ivory figurines. The women, at least. Our men were not beautiful. They were rawboned and hairy, squat rather than petite. Their wings were stubby and earth-colored instead of silver or striped. The fennecs tolerated them only for purposes of propagation. Only until they learned that human males can also impregnate us. Not just any male, to be sure. Our bodies have subtle differences from those of human women. Often we must take a host of lovers to find the one man who can profit us. But the fennecs are patient. They prize us all the more because they must take pains with us. Wait for the fulfillment of our beauty. When we first become Uglies, they put us to work in the fields and the kitchens; in other words, keep us out of the way. When they can no longer endure our proximity, they leave us in a city like Jericho to emerge and profit. In my case, Chackal selected your house because it is relatively isolated on the walls—he had seen it, and Ram, from the desert. Aspen accompanied him when he brought me there. She sprinkled the air with powdered oleander leaves to induce a heavy sleep in your mother. Then she stole Ram from his bed. He was the hostage for my well-being."

"Has he been well treated?"

She said quietly, "He is somewhat changed. Not hurt, you understand, but—well, it has been a year. He's lived a sixth of his life in Honey Heart."

"He lived five-sixths of it with me."

"Of course he did, my dear. He hasn't forgotten you. You'll see him shortly."

"When they left you in his place, did you know what to expect?"

"When an Ugly is left in a human city, she is touched with forgetfulness by her Master. Otherwise, willingly or not, she might betray the location of Honey Heart. Only toward the end, only when she has profited, does she remember everything."

"The day we went into the oasis. Did you know Chackal was waiting for you?"

"He called me, I suppose. But I mistook his voice for a simple longing to leave the city with you. It was that too, of course."

"And when he came back with us?"

"He fascinated me. I wanted to keep him with me. I didn't know why."

"Can't he hear you now—your thoughts, I mean?"

"If he chooses, he can hear them at any time. But the power of a Master is limited by distance. And the concentration required is very great, even close at hand. Besides, he says that my body is much more beautiful than my thoughts, which seem to him unkempt. Rebellious. They remind him of a shattered mosaic. He has always mistrusted me. That's why he called me into the desert from your house. To insinuate himself as naturally as possible into your household and watch over my movements. He knew when I was ready to emerge—it is always the last day of our fifteenth year —and he wished to be with me to make sure that I profited as soon as possible. With most Wingers, it is a natural inclination. Both to pleasure and profit. But Chackal sensed my resistance, my rebelliousness. When I gave myself to Zeb and Salmon, it was as I told you. I was compelled. Chackal was in the room both times, you recall. Even so, I fought him. He had to will me into a kind of dream in which it seemed that— someone else—was making love to me. And then he led me back to Honey Heart."

"But why? You had only emerged the week before!" She patted my hand. "Bard, Bard! Why else unless

99

I had profited? Chackal knew at once. They always do."

Zeb was starting to blush through his day's growth of beard. He looked at me as if to say: Well, if somebody has to be the father, wouldn't you rather it was me than that big-footed Wanderer? After all, I'm one of the family.

"It wasn't you, Zeb."

He looked crestfallen. It was Big Feet after all.

"It might have been you. But you were ill at ease, I think."

"You weren't my first," he snorted. "When I was a shepherd—"

"It wasn't proficiency you lacked, it was inclination. You wondered how Bard would feel. You'll remember I had to coax and importune you. You've never known what to make of me, have you, my dear?"

"No," he admitted. "I'm more at home with a camel. They aren't so mysterious."

"I have no mystery, Zeb. Men call a woman mysterious to avoid the trouble of understanding her."

"What will happen to Salmon's child?" My interest was much more than avuncular.

"If it's a girl, she will grow up like me. Littley, Ugly, Winger. Perhaps Comely."

"If it's a boy?"

"Boys are treated differently. They never have wings. Not since the males of our own race were eliminated. A boy is human in every respect except that he's likely to be hideous from birth to death. He's an Ugly all his life."

"But the fennecs don't like ugliness."

"No. And ugly boys are suffocated soon after birth."

"They are not going to suffocate our—your—boy!"

"I hope it will be a girl. If not—" She gave a sad shrug.

"Will the fennecs do it?" My question was hardly more than a gasp.

"Killing is too untidy for them. Uglies do the job. They suffocate the baby with a velvet cushion and bury him in a little casket of beaten gold. Our women are very adept at such things. When the time came to kill the male ancestors of our race, it was their own wives who smothered them in their sleep, bathed them with myrrh, and laid them out in linen."

"If the boy isn't ugly?" I had seen no boys at all in Honey Heart.

"If he's truly beautiful—well, you'll see for yourself."

"And Jericho is one of your spawning grounds." I shuddered.

"Profiting grounds, we are taught to say. The fennecs prefer euphemisms for natural functions. Yes, Jericho is distinctly promising. If it develops, the fennecs of Honey Heart may use it exclusively. All of us here speak Canaanite, but lately we have been drilled in the special Jerichite dialect, which is softer and slower than, say, the speech of Ai or Jerusalem. In other cities, the fennecs have had some bad failures. Sometimes the Uglies were stoned to death as demons, in spite of the hostages. Sometimes, as in Sodom and Gomorrah, the women emerged from their chrysalises only to find that their charms were not appreciated by the right sex. In Jericho, however, my own experience was considered a triumph. No one ever threatened to stone me, and there was no lack of accommodating males. Still, the fate of my predecessor, Silver Fire, is remembered as a warning. Steps must be taken to see that future Uglies fare as well as I did. A network of tunnels has been dug under the city. You came here through one of them. Thus, the Masters can remain close to their Servitors. Guard and guide them. They can actually visit them if contact seems to be dimming. To facilitate such visits, the fennecs mean to intrude themselves into the very life of the city. Become pets, if necessary. Accustom the Jerichites to their presence. Mingle with the other animals. Such masquerading is like a game for them. Dirt-Going, they call it."

"You've never thought of rebelling? Catching Chackal off guard and killing him? If enough of you killed their Masters—"

"Often," she said. "But the others would never join me. They don't really want to revolt. Once they've emerged, they're not unhappy in Honey Heart. Like the cats in Egypt, they've grown accustomed to being kept, scolded, pampered, displayed. If it weren't for my unkempt thoughts and the fact that I met you, I might be content myself." She smiled. "But I did meet you, and my thoughts are downright tumultuous."

"And magnificent." I reached out my hand to touch her.

I felt her stiffen under my fingers. I saw her features die into a mask. She might have been marblized by the stare of a Gorgon.

I did not need to look at the door to see who had entered the room, but I looked all the same, willing the force of my hatred to freeze him in his tracks, as he had frozen Rahab. His entrance was more assured than dramatic. He settled languorously on the moss beside the brazier. Firelight caressed his fur to a smoldering russet. He felt no need to posture for those whom he already possessed, and lest there should be any doubt about possession, two young Wingers stationed themselves inside the door: sinewy women for so delicate a race; warriors in short leather tunics with blowguns in their belts.

Rahab began to speak. The marble had flowed to life; one spell, at least, had been exorcised. The words she spoke were the notes of a lyre, measured and melodious, but the lyrist's invisible fingers controlled her strings.

"I am Moondust's Master. I will speak through her."

"Tell him—" I began to Rahab.

"Speak directly to me. I understand what you say." His florid sentences were those of a pharaoh addressing his court. "I know the tongues of the desert and the tongues of the city. Jerichite and Egyptian, Phoenician and Cretan. I can speak with the earth-dwelling fox or the mountain-dwelling eagle. When the viper sways his tongue, I listen and comprehend, and the lizard which runs like a flame withholds no secrets from me."

"Where is my brother?"

"I have sent for him."

"You'll let us take him back to Jericho?"

"He would not choose to accompany you. Even should you return."

"We're prisoners then?"

"Invaders cannot expect to roam Honey Heart at will."

"Invaders? Two unarmed men!"

"And a beast of utmost repugnance. Unarmed, yes. But with mischievous intent."

"Our intent was to find Rahab, my sister."

103

"The kinship you claim is somewhat whimsical. Moon-dust will return to Jericho in her own time. In my own time. But we have visitors—"

The arrival of the children was like all the wind-bees in the room tinkling at the same time. They flowed rather than walked, and their voices and laughter were one silvery sound. I had the disquieting thought that they were exquisite artifacts, manufactured, polished, and now displayed.

Once in the room, they looked around them without shyness and gracefully bowed, first to Chackal and then to Rahab. They seemed respectful of Chackal but not frightened of him. He raised his head as if to say: Advance to greet our guests.

They approached Zeb and me with decorous steps and placid smiles. They wore tunics to their knees; tiny coral sea gulls fluttered on anklets and brace-lets. One of them carried a bow over her shoulder and a quiver of arrows on her back. The other two looked as if they had never drawn a bow and certainly never dirtied their gowns. I was not sure if they were Littlies or human children, snatched from the Sun World as hos-tages.

One of them said, "We bring you greetings, strangers. Is it well in the Sun World?" For a child who appeared to be no more than six or seven, she spoke with remark-able assurance.

"Well enough," I said. I was staring at the girl with the bow. I said to her, not to the speaker, "Was that your world before you came here?"

The speaker answered my question. "The Masters tell us so. We do not remember it, nor wish to."

The girl with the bow returned my stare and seemed

about to speak. Her hair was such a red as I saw only when I looked in the mirror. True, she wore it in a decidedly feminine style, flaring over her shoulders and looping over her forehead in three meticulous curls. But it was she who carried the bow, and proudly, as if it were more than a pretty pastime for her.

"Ram?" I asked.

His face seemed to catch fire with surprise and fear and, I thought, affection. I caught him in my arms. For an instant I felt his hands, small but strong, clasp behind me and press into my back. Then he began to hit me. Aghast, I dropped my arms.

"Ram, you don't remember me! It's Bard, your brother!"

He stumbled backward out of my reach.

"Did he wrinkle your gown?" one of the girls piped. "He's an old clumsy." And the other girl: "The big one looks like a bear. Someone ought to trim him!"

Their liquid voices had become shrill with excitement, and Chackal, who till now had watched us with bright, fervid eyes, was starting to look pained.

Zeb bristled: "I eat little girls who insult my friends!"

The two little girls squealed with delectable terror and fled for the door. Ram called after them, "Wait for me! They're picking mushrooms in the fields. Let's get a cart and bring one back with us."

"He has forgotten you," said Chackal (through Rahab). "In a year, a child forgets much."

"How to be a boy?"

"He was a rough child when he came. Beautiful, yes. But he fought us constantly. His lovely features were marred by tears and anger. We were patient teachers,

105

however. You saw the result. He is now a paragon of obedience."

Anger has been called a conflagration or an inundation; a fire or a flood. In me, it was both at the same time. I must have tried to kill him. I must have run at him like a stampeding elephant (a baby elephant, to be sure). Zeb intercepted me. His arms were those of a shepherd, gently implacable.

I stomped savagely on his foot.

"No, Bard," he whispered. "They'll kill you." He had seen the guardians raise their blowguns.

"All right," I gasped. "You can let me go." He released me by degrees but kept his hand on my arm, in case I changed my mind.

Chackal fixed me with a look of lofty disapproval. I had never thought of animals as having such a range of physical expression. Sadness, joy, or anger, yes, but few subtleties. A fennec, though, could convey at least the equivalent of every human emotion. A raised head, a flick of a paw, a narrowing of eyes, and he acknowledged, dismissed, disapproved.

"You are much as your brother used to be. Contentious and impetuous. But he was not beyond domestication. Both of you are delicious to the eye. Your hair is an asset. A rarity in Honey Heart. It is rather like the color of our fur. And your body is delicately fashioned for a boy. Not like the Jerichites, fat and loutish." He looked at Zeb: "Or hirsute. Or like those hulking Wanderers, the one called Salmon, for example. I found his feet insufferable. But you, my dear—I believe we can prepare you for a place with us."

VIII

HE DELIBERATED. He delivered a quick bark which
sounded distinctly like an "Ah!" Rahab understood him,
his thought if not his speech, and swept from the room
on his errand. I never got over expecting her to fly.
I have said before that she seemed to walk in music.
I might have said celestial music. The harmonies of
wind and gull and sky-tossed foam.

Chackal followed her with a proprietary gaze. "Have
you ever seen so splendid a creature?" he seemed to ask.
It was our one moment of rapport, our one agreement,
though her splendor to me meant admiration; to him possession. He was the connoisseur who displays an ivory
scabbard from the land of Punt or an ebony jewel casket, paneled in gold and blue faience, from the boudoir
of an Egyptian princess. Rahab existed solely to feed his
pride. Should she ever become flawed, he would despise
her; dispose of her. There were no aged women in Honey
Heart. I did not have to be told what had happened
to them.

In the silence of Rahab's absence, he closed his eyes,
leaned to the brazier, luxuriated in the warmth. His
fur stiffened and prickled. The scent of nard, musky
and aromatic, laded the air.

As for myself, I felt as if I had drunk hemlock.
I was locked in the gloom of Rahab's captivity. Zeb,

who had a gift for silence, also knew when to speak. He shook me with his awkward, solid, and altogether lovable arm.

"Never mind, Bard. It will be all right." Simple words, threadbare words. But to me they spoke with eloquence: It will be all right because I, Zeb, your friend, am with you. My strength, though somewhat limited in a land where animals are cruel instead of men, is yours for all it is worth, and my love, though inarticulate and clumsy, is unshakable, a shepherd's staff against the wolves.

Deciding to be merely sixteen, I burrowed into his arms like a strayed lamb. From the moment of her emergence, I had lost Rahab as a sister. Whatever she had become, phantom, temptress, Servitor, she was no longer warm and close and comfortable. I had found Ram only to lose him again and, this time, I feared, for good. I needed the love which is constant and familiar but not fleshly; which enfolds but does not enflame; friendlove, brotherlove, fatherlove: a bearskin coverlet on a cold night, cracknels hot in the oven.

"Zeb," I said. "How did I get you into this?"

"Sixteen asses couldn't have kept me in Jericho," he grinned. "Plus a camel. And that's one stubborn animal."

The fennec snorted. Our chatter had interrupted his repose. Barbarians, he seemed to say. Have you no regard for the solemnities of silence? Fortunately, Rahab reappeared with a circular tray of black obsidian and two silver cups shaped like mushrooms.

"You are honored," Chackal resumed through his spokesman. "A Comely to wait upon you! Usually such tasks are reserved for the more menial Wingers."

I accepted a cup with trepidation. The contents bubbled and swirled with an unidentifiable opalescent liquid. However, I had neither eaten nor drunk since the tunnel. Hunger was a fox cub in my stomach and thirst was sand in my throat. My physical needs outweighed my discretion. I raised the cup to my lips, but Zeb caught my hand.

"We don't know what it is."

"It is a wine on which we pride ourselves here in Honey Heart. It is blended from a certain choice mushroom dissolved in the nectar of moonflowers. Mushrooms for body, nectar for bouquet. You need have no reservations. It will quench your thirst and solace your hunger. I might add that it will be your *only* repast. If you disdain our best, you shall go without our least."

Zeb emptied his cup with one swift gulp. If it was poison, he wanted to make the test. He closed his eyes and tensed as if expecting paralysis or a paroxysm.

A smile eased over his features. "Good," he sighed, leaning back among the jonquils and lolling like a bear in peppermint.

He was right. I might have been drinking liquid moonbeams. Their fire, though cool, seemed to infuse and suffuse my limbs. Surely I had begun to glow like the walls of Honey Heart! I looked at Zeb to see if he too had grown phosphorescent.

He raised his cup to me. "Sure beats goat milk."

"Why aren't you glowing?" I scolded, thinking him very careless. But soon I began to feel confused instead of suffused. Zeb and his jonquils had retreated into a yellow mist. Chackal was still in the room—Rahab too —I ought to make conversation with them, compliment the wine, admire the mushroom cup which I was holding with some difficulty. But my tongue felt as if it were hibernating; it refused to budge except in a mumble:

"Forgive me." I felt enormously apologetic. I was the guest who had abused his host's hospitality. "The journey must have tired me."

"The wine has made you drowsy."

"But I only d-drank one cup."

"It was a special kind of cup. I told you that it was made from one of our mushrooms. It was made from the one which you of the Sun World call the Death Cup."

"That's fatal," I said in a matter of fact voice. I did not feel in the least imperiled. The lights had sunk into shadows; the wind-bees trembled in another Den. Chackal, Rahab, Zeb? Let them stay if they wished and become a part of my dream. Let them move, gesture, speak, but they would be to me as swimmers seen by a murex diver from the bottom of the sea. This talk of Death Cups—I could hear it, muffled by liquid fathoms, but it came from the surface, and in my world it was—what?—an echo, a whisper, a memory.

"It is fatal," I repeated. The words amused instead of alarmed me. I spoke each word with separate emphasis. "It . . . is . . . fatal."

"Not in small quantities such as you have just imbibed. First you will sleep. When you awaken, you will remain tractable for several hours. At no time will you feel pain. You see, dear boy, there is a certain small subtraction which we must make from your charming person. If you are going to stay with us, you must respect our sensibilities. You are—how old?—sixteen. Soon, an unsightly growth will deface your chin and cheeks. We shall save you from having to trim, perfume, or shave it. We shall prevent it. Your friend, needless to say, is beyond redemption. It is more than a matter of excessive hair. He is too clumsy and too—*muscular*. But you—you shall soon be fit to associate with our Comelies. Our dear Moondust—your Rahab—shall be your affectionate companion, a sister again as when you first knew her. She will trouble you no longer with her womanly sensualities."

Zeb muttered, "What are you going to do with the muscular friend?"

The fennec paused like a rhetorician before his climax. Posed, I should say. "We are going to return the friend to his beast. Shut them together in the same compound. The beast has not been fed since his arrival. He must forage for himself. We shall test the extent of his affection for his master. Will it be one day or two before he decides that appetite is stronger than devotion?"

I seemed to be lying on a white stone under blue water. Truth said: It is the walls of the room which are blue—blue tufa rock. And the light which shines from the candelabrum above you, a circle of slowly revolving butterflies, each holding a candle, absorbs the tints of the walls until it seems to swim bluely about the room. It is not a weight of water which holds you down but shackles around your hands and ankles; and around your waist, a metal band like those which the Cretan girls wear to limit their waistlines and accentuate their breasts. Truth said: You are a prisoner awaiting a subtraction. Truth said: Your friend Zeb has been placed in a compound with a ravenous hyena.

But the haze, the rotating candelabrum, the sleep in my veins. . . . Truth existed in other rooms, for other men. I was immaterialized. I was liquefied into a blue euphoria and out of time. . . .

I smiled up at the two Wingers who seemed to have fluttered down from the surface like flying fish, wind-clean and water-bright. It was Manna and Luna. Manna held a square tray with folded linen cloths, a set of diminutive tongs, and a knife like a miniaturized sickle with a sharp curved end.

I was not in the least embarrassed by my nudity. Under the sea, who needed a tunic? "You may finish bathing me," I said to them. "There's plenty of water." I tried to raise my hand to gesture the enormity of the amount and felt, with neither surprise nor anger, my gracious imprisonment.

The caress of their eyes was almost physical, like the tendrils of an angelfish. Their look held a sensual appreciation which warmed me even in my cool quiescence. Perhaps, I thought, I *do* have animal magnetism. The pleasant thing about thoughts in my present condition was that I either avoided them or I gave them a happy turn; they were rainclouds which I sent scudding across the sky and out of sight or else evaporated with sunlight.

"Poor dear," said Luna. "It seems so wasteful. He quite took your fancy, didn't he, Manna?"

Manna nodded. "It makes one want to go out again, doesn't it? Remember the Hittite captain in Gezer?"

"Uncouth but unforgettable. And doubly accommodating. I wouldn't have my Master hear me, but I *like* the hairy ones. This little fellow's friend looked fine to me."

Suddenly she was all professional. Her look became appraising rather than appreciative, as if she were staking me out for the instruments on the tray. Naïvely I thought that I must have grown some hair on my chest and she meant to give me a shave. I started to say: No, you mustn't do that. I've waited sixteen years to grow that hair. Maybe you can transplant some onto my face. Then I saw that Chackal had entered the room with two other fennecs and Rahab.

I observed with no particular curiosity that Rahab was holding herself like a warrior on guard, rigid and unsmiling. One could imagine a spear in her hand or a bow across her shoulder.

"Rahab," I began. I wanted to tell her to merge with the current; to flow, to waft, to glide. Above all, to relax the rigidity of her features. Perhaps "wanted" is too strong a word; I did not really want anything except to dream.

The two strange fennecs took up stations behind Luna and Manna. I gathered that they were the Wingers' Masters, come to supervise them. They were slighter than Chackal, a little less glossy, certainly less assured. There was no scent of nard about them, and their eyes were more furtive than commanding. If there were hierarchies in Honey Heart, Chackal was a leader and these were subordinates.

Apparently Luna and Manna were capable of managing the instruments without the supervision of their Masters. Chackal did not intend to share the occasion with other fennecs. He issued a series of quick, incisive barks. A petulant whine, a sniff of grudging acquiescence, and the unwanted Masters left the room.

His authority established, Chackal addressed Manna and Luna through Rahab. "I suggest that you wait until after the subtraction to resume your gossiping. Do you

113

want the wine to lose its effect? He can be quite vicious, I suspect, even in shackles. Manna, slide the brazier beside his couch. There now, Luna can reach it with the tongs."

Eunuchs, like jesters, astrologers, and physicians, flourish in almost every court, in almost every country, around the Great Green Sea. Their high-pitched voices, their fluttery movements, their beardless cheeks are recognized, ridiculed, and reviled from Egypt to Knossos. Young, they are often delicate and beautiful. Old, they become smooth, plump, and oily like hogs fattened for the table, and as cruel and furtive as crocodiles. I found myself cataloguing the attributes of a eunuch with the objectivity of a lexicographer. Then, as if I were granted a window through the haze, I saw myself as a eunuch. Not even the power of the wine could prevent a momentary sobering.

Luna, confident of my torpor, smiled and prepared to begin the subtraction. The silver sickle descended like a malicious dragonfly. I heard the sizzling of the coals in the brazier and knew how she would cauterize my wound. I heard the throaty purring of Chackal, who had turned his head to avoid the sight of blood but who had no wish to hide his excitement. I strained upward with a swift, violent spasm and winced as the shackles bit into my flesh.

The sickle hesitated, a dragonfly poised in flight. From which direction to attack? Slowly or with one irrevocable slash?

"Shin," I prayed. No, he protected sheep. "Astarte," I prayed, "who likes lusty men. Mother, wife, and mistress, are you going to allow this appalling theft, this inexcusable waste, this diminution of your own power and authority and fertility?"

Then, the flash of resumed flight.

I shut my eyes. Figuratively, I girded my loins. I—

"Aieee!"

Yahweh preserve me, I thought (no need for Astarte now). I already sound like a girl!

But the cry had come from Luna and not from me. The sickle protruded crookedly from her shoulder, like a broken twig. Someone had struck her hand and her weapon, up and away from me and against her own body. Her lips quivered uncertainly between sobs and recriminations.

Chackal's expression was indecipherable. He looked like Anubis, the jackal god of the Egyptians, frozen in stone. Doubtless he was reasserting his power over Rahab. She too seemed stone; or Lot's wife, turned to salt. But flushed with what angers and ardors?

"What did he do with Rahab?" I asked the question with an aching head but a clear brain. I had struggled out of the protective, imprisoning depths of my intoxication, burned my lungs with the airs of truth, vomited over the side of the couch, and waited fretfully for Chackal's return. It was Manna who returned, however, and looking as if she had a secret to share.

"I hope my Máster isn't in. I simply had to tell you about *your woman*. Moondust is the first Winger in years to disobey a Master. To be *able* to disobey, even for an instant. We thought he was going to have her put away at once. In fact, Luna kept wailing that she was about to die and Moondust ought to be suffocated slowly and with a coarse goatskin instead of a cushion! Her

Master arrived on the scene and exchanged some indignant barks with Chackal, but Chackal sent him scurrying and turned his thoughts to Moondust. At first she tried to queen it—you know how the Comelies are, even with their Masters. Stuck on themselves. Then she gave a start and we knew he had said something terribly decisive. As soon as he left the room, we made her repeat what he had told her. We said it was the least she could do after all the trouble she'd caused, though Luna's wound was really just a scratch. It seems that Chackal had *liked* Moondust's rebellion. He thought her gesture the most artistic, the most delicious, he had ever seen. He compared it to music. Can you imagine? He said it was like a trumpet blast—sudden and rhythmic and electrifying. Unerring and unnerving. He called it the stroke of a master. Or mistress, I should say. In short, he had decided to let her compete in the Wind War. Usually the Comelies don't participate. It would be such a waste. At least, the Masters think so. Personally, I don't know what else they're good for. Anyway, he's going to enter Moondust. He said that anyone who could move so fast to help *you* can take care of herself in the air. And do you know what? If she wins, he's going to let you go! You and your friend. His beast didn't devour him, by the way. You'll both be returned to the Sun World."

"Wind War?" I stammered. She had inundated me with revelations; I badly needed some explanations, one at a time.

"In the Wind Well, of course. I expect you saw it when you came out of the tunnel."

"But Rahab can't fly!"

"She'll have her Moth like the rest. And her slasher.

It'll be the best War we've ever had. A Comely fighting for her lover! Fancy having her die for you. What a sacrifice! Chackal will probably bury her in a gold casket, with you at her feet, holding asphodels. The Masters can be terribly sentimental."

"And you say Zeb wasn't hurt?"

"His devoted beast crawled in a corner and closed its eyes. To avoid temptation, I expect. Now, the beast has been washed and fed, and your friend is waiting for you back in Chackal's Den. And tomorrow—the Wind War! By the way, Chackal said I could remove your bonds. You're to lie here and rest till someone comes for you. You're not to walk by yourself. The wine has aftereffects. I expect you would fall and break a leg and have to be carried to the War." With a squeal of anticipation—for the War, I trusted, not my breaking a leg—she left me to my aching head and smarting wrists.

I felt as if my skull were being ground under a pestle. I almost welcomed the distraction of pain, however. My forebodings for Rahab were not pleasant. She had rescued me from subtraction. Now she was going to fight for me in the Wind War. Was there no end to her trials? And was I worthy of them—a red-haired runt with a bad disposition?

When I heard the footsteps, I thought that the some-one promised by Manna had come to escort me to Chack-al's Den. But they were secretive steps. I raised my-self on one shoulder and looked into a pair of enormous green eyes surmounted by a profusion of meticulously teased and vividly red curls. The owner was waiting for me to speak. He was, I think, waiting for me to scold him.

"Ram," I said. "I've missed you." The green eyes filled with tears. "Remember the sow with the reddish bristles? The one you brought home your—your last night? Her master didn't eat her after all. She's still in Jericho."

He knelt beside me and pressed his face against my shoulder. I felt him shake with sobs. Perhaps I should say that we exchanged sobs.

"I knew you all the time," he quavered. "But they told me to say I didn't. Did they hurt you, Bard?"

"No. Have they hurt you, Rhadamanthus?" I had to say his whole name for once. I needed the full four syllables to express my love.

"They punished me at first. The Uglies whipped me when I wouldn't behave. And you know what?" He wrecked his elaborate coiffure with a thrust of his hand.

"What?"

"I hate them, Bard. All of them except Moondust."

He gave me a quick, wet kiss and fled through the door.

IX

IT WAS MORNING. There was no sun to rise and dissipate the twilight which cobwebbed the oval windows, but the sounds of dawn were sweet in the air. From far away came the barking of foxes in the compounds;

118

deeper, throatier than that of the fennecs. Barkings of sheer animal exuberance and not the carefully articulated sounds of a reasoned and reasonable language. Foxes waiting to be fed and harnessed to their chariots. Directly under us, the Uglies were chattering in the kitchen as they stoked the ovens and drew wine from jars or goatskins. Normal sounds, you would think. How else should a day begin except with preparations and anticipations? But this was an abnormal day.

I buried my head among the jonquils, lessened my body into the silky leaves, and willed my thoughts to march backwards in time to the house on the wall, the clay animals, Rahab plain again, safe and predictable. It was useless. She refused to stay in the past.

Zeb slumbered beside me with annoying ease. Having spent much of yesterday in a compound with an underfed hyena, he needed his sleep. At the same time, I needed his company.

"Zeb."

Like most shepherds (or onetime shepherds) he slept heavily when there were no wolves in the neighborhood and no sheep to guard. I felt slighted. Was I not a part of his flock, his favorite and most deserving sheep?

I gave his arm an insistent yank. "Zeb!"

The arm retaliated by rolling me off the hillock and onto the moss. He growled, swept the hair out of his eyes, and rubbed them with his big hands. As soon as he removed his hands, the hair resumed its waterfall and his eyes peered out as if from a cave.

"I wanted company," I explained from the moss. He staggered over to the pool and held his head under the water for so long that I was ready to start resuscitation.

"You knocked me down," I whimpered, trying to look wounded.

"Feed me and I'll make conversation."

"There's some food over there." I pointed to a round, three-legged table which, along with a chest of blond palm wood, had been brought into the room while we slept.

He appropriated a bunch of grapes, which he proceeded to eat not singly but in threes and fours.

"They're out of season," I remarked. "In the Sun World, they aren't due for months. I imagine you'll get indigestion." It was no use. My small talk could not evade the threat of large disaster. "I wonder where Rahab is. I wonder when the Wind War will start."

He dropped a half-denuded bunch of grapes and laid a sticky arm over my shoulder. "I think Rahab is going to win. Has she ever failed you? Yesterday she saved you from being subtracted. Today she's going to win your freedom in the War."

"But there's nothing I can do to help her. She's always doing things for *me*."

"You're in her country. She knows the ground. Besides, she's not one of our simpering little things—big things, I ought to say—from Jericho. If they can card flax and paint their cheeks, they think they're women. Rahab's a fighter. I say let her do for you."

"Well," I said, "if we're going to be done for, we'd better eat a big breakfast." I joined him in finishing the grapes—the few that were left—followed them with milk, manna, and fox cheese, and then explored the chest. Its contents had been selected with care. A loincloth for me, trim and tight in the Cretan style, with a pouch in front for coins and daggers, and decorated with red dolphins gamboling through a green sea. Sandals with clasps like flying fish. A signet ring, a carnelian incised with an octopus. For Zeb, an ankle-length tunic embroidered with sheep, goats, asses, and camels browsing among clover. It was evident that those who had selected the garments wished to hide as much as possible of Zeb and show as much as possible of me. It was also evident that we were being exploited for what you might call our aesthetic possibilities. The Masters—namely, Chackal—had decided that, like bits of colored tile, the Cretan exile and the priest who had been a shepherd would add their exotic colors to the mosaic of the Wind War.

Finally, there was a comb of nacre and a coral unguent jar containing a paste of nard. I recognized here the unmistakable handiwork of Chackal. We were his creatures, living by his sufferance and by the skill of his more exalted creature, Rahab. We would anoint our hair with the nard which was his own distinctive scent.

"I refuse to grease myself like a whore from Gezer," said Zeb.

I dipped my fingers into the paste and rubbed it liberally in my hair. "Rahab is going to fight in the sky. The least we can do is please the Masters on the ground. Now comb your hair!" I thrust the comb into his hand.

With a grimace, he disseminated some nard through his mane and struggled to admonish his locks with the comb, which snapped almost at once. He looked smug.

"I tried, Bard, but my hair resents interference."

Then they came for us. . . .

Our escorts were Luna and Manna. Luna was not her loquacious self of yesterday. She was nursing her wounded shoulder and looking put upon at having to conduct us to the War. She refused to brighten even when Zeb reminded her that, as a priest, he knew the rudiments of medicine. Would she like him to take a look at the shoulder? No, she would not. He would probably infect her with a demon of scrofula from his beast.

Manna, however, rose to the occasion. "You'll see us all at our best," she preened. "Best clothes and best manners. Everybody outdoes herself for the Wind War." She tilted her face to its most becoming angle and shook her hips to show how liquidly they flowed with her tunic of oleander-pink.

Other best clothes and manners shimmered on the street we had entered from Chackal's Den. The grass bent noiselessly beneath a hundred sandals and, every few seconds, the wheels of a chariot, a canopied affair, its single occupant a Master ensconced on a plush cushion. His Servitor walked beside him with a thorn-tongued whip which she cracked over the heads of four large foxes. The Masters looked superbly indifferent to their surroundings. The destination and not the journey concerned them.

Two of the Servitors made the mistake of falling into a conversation. "I'm betting sixteen ambers on Rahab!" one of them piped. Her Master exerted an instant rebuke. Without changing his position, he jerked her up as if by invisible reins, and thenceforth she watched the road and the foxes.

"Poor Hyacinth," said Manna. "Now she won't be allowed to bet at all. Maybe it's just as well. Moondust is a long shot."

"And where is *your* Master?" Zeb asked. The girl's chatter annoyed him. He wanted to watch the foxes.

"Our own Masters—Luna's and mine—released us to look after you. They're riding with friends."

"Released us? Ordered us!" Luna corrected. She flexed her arm and gave a whimper. "Never mind. I doubt I could hold a whip, much less manage a team."

Manna was not sympathetic with sore shoulders; not on a holiday. She pointed to one of the buildings ahead of us, a large orange sphere atop a cylindrical base.

"A school," she explained. "For the Uglies who are about to go out." Row upon row of circular windows ran around the walls, and several Uglies were peering down at us with plump, forlorn faces.

"Can't they attend the Wars?"

"They can't leave the building. It's too near time for them to go out, and they have a lot to learn."

"What?" Zeb wanted to know.

"What to do when they emerge."

"I thought they forgot everything," I said. "Like Rahab."

"They forget Honey Heart, yes. But their training stays with them. When they seem to be acting through instinct, they're really remembering their lessons."

"Training for *what?*" Zeb persisted.

"You're a man. You ought to know."

"I'm a country boy."

"How to select tunics which conceal and reveal in the right proportion. How to apply kohl and carmine."

"What else?"

"How to compete with the local harlots without

looking like them. The temptation, as I well remember, is to overdo things once you emerge. Too much pleasuring. That's no way to profit, is it, Luna?"

"Who wants to profit her first week out?" snapped Luna, with an obvious slur on Rahab. "I always say: Pleasure before profit."

One of the Uglies leaned out of a window and waved her hand. Her eyebrows met across a nose which could only be called squalid. "Can't we borrow one of your friends for today's lesson? All day long, nothing but papyrus rolls and pictures and diagrams. I never could get anything out of a scroll!"

Manna shook an admonishing finger. "You know what we say, girls. Practice makes profit. I speak as one who knows." She turned back to us. "And that double building across the way. One globe piled on top of another. That's the Suffocatorium. Ugly male babies are suffocated in the top and cremated in the bottom. Then their ashes are buried in silver urns and given to their mothers. It's the kindest thing under the circumstances. That way, everybody is spared, and the urns are very decorative. And there, the rufous building. That's where the Pregies are kept. Luna and I will go there when we lose our figures." She lifted her head to erase the intimation of a double chin. "It won't be long, I'm afraid."

"Speak for yourself," Luna grumbled.

"And after you give birth?"

"We'll go out again—if we get our looks back."

"If you don't?"

"And the big white building opposite. That's where you were yesterday. We call it the House of Subtraction. And there, just inside the wall—"

It was a low, gently rounded building which hugged

the earth like the hood of a mushroom without a stem. We could hear a clatter of looms and a medley of voices which rasped and whistled and seemed neither human nor animal. I almost collided with Zeb when I saw a multiplicity of legs, hairy and jointed, scuttle past the window.

"Those are the Silk Spinners," Manna said. "In the East, they use worms. But spiders are more artistic."

And so we left the town and came, across a field of asphodels, to the place of the Wind War. . . .

The Wind Well was not like the bull ring I remembered from Crete, the amphitheater whose seats fell, tier after stone tier, into an arena which was adjoined by bull pens. On the contrary, it seemed a natural formation, a small crater whose inner walls descended in three terraces, like huge round stair steps, and then abruptly sank into a pit whose bottom was hidden by bubbling mists. The rich soil of the terraces seemed to have flowered into a young woodland, with copses of blackberry bushes, clumps of palm trees, clusters of rhododendrons, and everywhere, mushrooms sprouting to a height of perhaps two feet. When you saw that many of the plants did not belong in the same season or the same climate—sun-loving palms beside sun-shy rhododendrons—you realized that the fennecs had once again improved on nature. The plants, even to the mushrooms, were artificial—woven, spun, welded, who could say? It was enough that they deceived the eye and mingled colors and shapes with that deceptive artistry which conceals art.

Only the pit was manifestly real. Not even Masters and Servitors could have created such a horror. I had

125

no doubt that it plunged into Sheol. Its black and ocher bubblings—jackal-colored, I thought—thinned to a clear transparency as they reached its rim and spewed in a wide wavering column to the roof of the cavern. Here was the vaunted Wind Well, the place of the Wars. One felt its heat. Heard its perpetual moan. Guessed its power to lift, rend, and crush. It seemed to dissipate itself in the roof of the cavern, which bristled with stalactites like sharp fir trees: an inverted forest.

Manna watched me with pride of possession. "It *is* horrendous, isn't it? Honey Heart's foremost spectacle. We have a theory about all those wailings you hear."

"Like yelping jackals."

"Exactly. The Well wasn't always quite so ferocious. When the fennecs first brought us here, it blew and whirled but it didn't wail. But every year since, it seems to get a little more fierce, a little more clamorous. Our Masters say that the souls of dead War-Riders linger in the Well. It's them you hear wailing and not jackals. They're angry because they lost the War, and sometimes they like to play tricks with the wind to make other Riders lose and come to join them. That's what the Masters say. I don't know about such things. But there's no doubt that the wind is—well, *alive.* That's the only word for it. You'll see what I mean when the War begins."

At the edge of the crater the Masters were stepping from their chariots onto a low mound exactly the height of their seats. From the mound, a network of paths serpentined down the slopes of the crater. Once the Masters had reached their seats on the third and lowest terrace, the Servitors unharnessed the foxes, drove them into a compound, and then found seats for themselves on the second terrace.

The thickets, copses, and glades had been designed not only to please the eye, but to afford a view both down toward the pit and up the walls of the Well. The mushrooms were the seats. The Masters generally chose to sit under them to protect their fur. A late-arriving fennec, who had set his heart on a particular glade, found every mushroom occupied by the members of the same family, and to heighten his disappointment, two little brothers were crowding under his favorite mushroom. The latecomer set up a barking—in this case, thought transference was not sufficiently dramatic—which soon had his Servitor fetching him the canopy from his chariot.

"Dust settles from the Well," Manna explained. "And later, there may be blood and debris. I spoiled a tunic last year."

They led us down a path strewn with brown leaves—artificial, though they crackled under our sandals—to the second level. (The first level, we were told, would be occupied by the Uglies after everyone else was seated; thus, no one would have to look at them when they arrived.) Seats had been reserved for us in the midst of a blackberry patch and shaded by palm trees. Though I was disconcerted by the conjunction of palms and blackberries, to say nothing of mushrooms, I had to admit that the mushrooms made comfortable seats—they were soft and porous and stuffed with a material which Manna called rubber—and our view was excellent in all directions. The trees shaded us but did not prevent our watching the Well, the sky, or the Servitors and human girls (and boys?) who shared the terrace with us. I spotted Ram with the two little girls who had been his companions in Chackal's Den. He grinned at me and mussed his hair.

"Don't stare at him," whispered Zeb. "You'll get him in trouble." Then, to divert attention, he plucked a blackberry and rolled it between his fingers. "Phoenician glass. I might have guessed."

It was I, though, who suffered from stares and not Ram. I suddenly felt as if I had forgotten to wear a tunic over my loincloth. Everyone was staring at me. Wingers on either side, particularly the Comelies, in spite of their chill detachment. Fennecs on the third level—for example, those two brothers under the same mushroom. Rude little cubs, I would have liked to box their ears! And yes, even the finally-arriving Uglies while they looked for seats.

"What is it? What's the matter with me?" I asked Manna.

"Enjoy your celebrity," she smirked, clearly enjoying hers. "You're the chief attraction next to Rahab. That's why Chackal had those seats saved for us. Everyone thinks that it was you who profited her. What's more, she's going to fight for you. You'll have to admit that the situation tingles with drama."

The crowd was discussing me as if I were deaf.

"That's the father? But he's so young and small! It took me twenty lovers to profit, and the twentieth was a big, lusty Hittite of mature years." (I felt a flush of pride at being credited with Salmon's achievement, but a pique of annoyance at the implication that virility is a matter of size.)

"They learn fast in Jericho. It's the tropical sun, I expect. Why else do you think Rahab wants to go back?"

Money was beginning to change hands: instead of the silver weights we used in Jericho, polished spheres of amber.

"Thirteen ambers on Rahab."

"*Fourteen* on Asphodel." The bettor was a Comely. I judged from her emphasis that she was not so much betting for Asphodel as against Rahab, whose beauty had made her enemies in her own class.

"But where are they? Where are the Riders? It's time to start."

"Where *is* she?" I demanded of Manna.

"You'll see her as soon as she arrives. Keep your eyes on the Moths." She pointed to a knotty, grassy projection which protruded over the pit from the lowest terrace. It was called the Blade. Even as I watched, the apparent grass, which was really a painted tarpaulin, was rolled back by a contingent of Servitors. The knots were revealed to be the Moths.

"Actually, they're a kind of kite. Their wings are silk, which is nailed to wooden frames. The antennae are rubber. The mandibles, though, are ivory and very sharp."

A Tiger Moth, with jaggedly striped wings of yellow and black and mandibles like fangs, fretted on the ground, dipping from side to side in the eddies from the Well.

"Notice his resemblance to that wicked, beautiful predator of the East," Manna said, as she thrust out her breasts and fluttered her own striped wings. "Stripes are a sign of passion, don't you know?"

"No, I didn't."

"Last year a Tiger Moth won the War. The Rider

129

was dead, though, when she reached the ground. From fright."

A Death's-Head Hawk Moth, unobtrusive with grays and sepias, rested out of the wind and looked as if he were sleeping on a giant blade of grass, but the skull on his back seemed to keep watch for him. An Emperor Moth, with four crowns emblazoned on his outstretched wings, waited like one accustomed to being feared and served, and the White Ermine Moth beside him could have been his queen: her wings were snow sprinkled with embers. And there, in the center of the Blade, crouched a Luna Moth whose pale green fire seemed borrowed from the moon. She was like a beached warship, tugged at by the tide; a curious marriage of repose and motion, grace and power.

"That will be Moondust's."

There were five of them, secured to cords controlled by winches, and five sinewy Wingers to control the winches. Four fennecs prowled importantly among the Moths, inspecting a winch, a wing, a cord, and parading themselves as conscientious Masters.

"Those are the Masters of the Riders. On hand to think instructions."

I looked in vain for Chackal. "But there are only four."

"Moondust asked to be on her own. We were surprised when Chackal agreed. He's really spoiling her. See, there he is just below us. That's my Master with him. They don't get along, but disagreements are forgotten on a day like this. Betting makes strange Denfellows."

The cheering began with the Uglies. Poor things, nobody wanted to look at them, but nobody had told

130

them that they should not be heard. The Riders had appeared on the first terrace, and the Uglies were crowding around them like puff balls encroaching upon five immaculate lotuses. The Riders did not want to be touched; four of them, at least. They drew in their wings and lifted their heads, and one of the four, a girl in lazuli, seemed to be holding her breath, as if she had caught the scent of ugliness and found it intolerable. The fifth, however, the slenderest and much the loveliest, cool but not cold, smiled to the Uglies and held out her hand. "I am not untouchable, I was once like you," she seemed to say.

"MOONDUST!"

The cry of the Uglies was an outcry; exultation and exaltation. Moondust, who had stepped from a thick, misshapen chrysalis to walk in beauty! Moondust, who did not scorn their ugliness! No one dared to take her hand, but one of them shyly brushed her wing and then retreated into the anonymity of the crowd.

Rahab paused. "I didn't see who touched me. But thank you."

The girl burst into tears.

All of the Riders wore leather tunics, armlets, leggings, and throat bands which differed only in color. Rahab's tunic was the red of wild strawberries. Alone among the Riders, she also wore leather boots tipped with electrum—the boots I had bought for her in Jericho—and a red fillet to bind her hair into a knot behind her head.

Manna amplified for me. "And see the rods they're carrying under their sashes? One end a hook, the other a blade? Those are called slashers."

"But what do they slash?"

"Each other," snapped Luna. "Now hush. I want to watch the War."

None of the Riders spoke as they stepped onto the Blade, and they walked in a column instead of abreast. It is not easy to talk to your intended victim or intending killer. The fennecs advanced to meet them; the Riders paired with their Masters to receive final instructions and encouragements. The fennecs were visibly nervous; their investment was immense, as Manna whispered. Each of them stood to lose the Servitor on whom he had expended years of patience and training. He had indulged her as a child, he had endured her as an Ugly, perhaps he had sent her out to profit and tolerated her subsequent pregnancy. Now, he must risk her in a war which could have only one victor—and one survivor. True, by risking so valuable a property he earned enormous prestige in the eyes of his people, and if his Rider won the War, he enjoyed the inestimable honor of having trained and guided her to victory. But prestige was a poor consolation for the fennec whose Den was no longer graced by a Servitor.

According to the rules of War, the five Riders were equally inexperienced. They had never flown the Moths, though they had been allowed to study them on the ground and to read a scroll written by their inventor. In the time before their bondage, Manna said, and before they had lost their power of flight, the Peoples of the Sea had fought their wars in the air and decimated their once sizable numbers to the few thousand entrapped by the fennecs. The Wind War had been designed to recapture the spectacle of those early aerial battles—their "militant pageantry," to use the designer's phrase.

The fennecs sniffed their Riders with pride and, if I could judge expressions from such a distance, with genuine affection and withdrew to the shelter of a palm-thatched canopy. The first Rider, dressed in jonquil-yellow, knelt to examine her craft, fingered the under-pinning, tilted the wings, tugged on the cord. She engaged in a quiet but lengthy conversation with the supervisor who would manage her cord. It soon became obvious that she was terrified. Her Master snorted with impatience and evidently jolted her with a sharp command. With the help of the supervisor, she dragged her White Ermine Moth to the edge of the pit. The craft rocked violently on the ledge. She threw herself onto its body, stretched her arms across its wings to grasp the ribs, and dug her feet into stirrup-like protuberances at the tail. The supervisor looked to the girl's Master, received his approval, and shoved the Moth toward the Well. Like an unseen Scylla, the winds reached out their multitudinous heads to snatch her into their maw.

The Moth sank briefly below the rim of the pit, then, caught by the winds, rose like a fishing boat in a water-spout; dipped and rolled and lurched; jerkily began to circle the spout even as it climbed. The Rider was paralyzed. Her fingers clawed into the silk of the wings. Her skin was not ivory but ashen. She made no attempt to control her craft. In the roar of the spout, she could not hear the well-meant admonitions of the crowd.

"Open your eyes, Oleander!"

"Lean to the right. More, more!"

But her Master reached her mind if not her ears. In the orange light, which sharpened and magnified every detail, even to the muscles knotted in her calves like clenched fists, even to the jonquil tunic limp with sweat, we could see her responding to his soundless commands; relaxing her body; blinking her eyes as if what she saw was too terrible to be seen except in glimpses, then locking them open in courageous obedience.

The cord unwound, the Moth circled and climbed. Oleander was beginning to gain confidence; beginning to experiment. She leaned to the right and her Moth responded with swiftness and power, a pirate's pentecoster instead of a fisherman's bark. So small a motion, so large a response! The craft after all was controllable, she seemed to decide. The air was conquerable. Her exhilaration reached the crowd. They—I—felt airborne. Controllers, conquerors, riding the aerial sea with a sturdy craft under us and limitless, lovely mist above us!

She loosened her feet from the stirrups, she inched forward along the body, and the ship was a moth again, a winged predator, its purpose not to fly but to do battle in flight, its mandibles dipping sharply as if to seize a morsel or rend an enemy. The Riders on the ground watched her with the agonized absorption of those who must learn from one performance and then perform for their lives. Rahab's face, particularly, was an anguish of concentration. You could see her willing the girl to mastery over her craft, the air, the crowd; wanting her to excel so that she, Rahab, could imitate and surpass her and then destroy her. For my sake.

She achieved a momentary balance; hung translucent between the roof and the ground. Time hung with her; she would poise forever, it seemed, athwart the stream, and no one would more or speak or even breathe, and the ravenous jackals of the wind would howl their hunger but howl in vain. Then she began to rock her Moth out of sheer bravado. In effect she was waving to those on the ground, challenging the other Riders, flaunting to them: "I took the first risk and won the first triumph. You on the ground, join me if you dare. But I have a start on you!"

But triumph was much more than riding a steady wind; it was anticipating the vagaries of the wind. Triumph was wariness and watchfulness and never, never the assured confidence of mastery. Even gods have been known to break their wings. In the time it takes to turn a parchment, the Moth rolled on its back. At first we thought that Oleander was performing an aerial feat, a maneuver to please and impress her Master and the crowd. But the feat belonged to the wind and not the Rider. She was taken by surprise; she was overtaken by the element she had briefly seemed to conquer.

"You see?" Manna whispered. "It's the spirits of the dead Riders. They can't stand for anyone to win."

Perhaps she was right. Even enlightened Cretans believe that spirits may be rejected by the Griffin Judge and barred from the Amber Palace of the Great Mother. Invisible and insatiable, they lurk in ruins or steal the bodies of the living or—who can say?—ride the whirlwind, ride the Wind Well.

Even as she turned, she managed to drive her feet into the stirrups. Wings billowing around her like a shroud, she seemed to be standing upside-down on the tail of her craft. Then, with the seemingly deliberate grace of a bull-wrestler, she appeared to step from the Moth and tread the air.

I expected her to plummet down the Well into the pit; her jonquils, bruised and wilted, recalled to earth. But waterspouts lift sailors as well as ships. Almost on a level with the riderless craft, which a Servitor desperately continued to unwind, she whirled upward toward the roof of the cave, clawing with frenzied fingers whenever the winds brought her close to the Moth, thrashing the currents like a swimmer . . . spinning inexorably upward to meet those hard, inflexible rocks, the stalactites of the inverted forest.

She fell to the ground with the remnants of her craft. Rider and Moth, separately broken, rejoined only in falling. Servitors hurried to remove her body.

The crowd was impatient. The fennecs were querulous. No more histrionics! There was a war to be fought. In quick succession the four remaining Moths were thrust upon the air.

At the sight of Rahab, the Uglies forgot their ugliness. They rolled from their seats and pressed to the edge of their terrace with a universal acclamation. The Comelies on the second level looked over their shoulders with raised eyebrows. They drew in their wings. They set up a cheer for all three of Rahab's opponents. But Zeb and I added our voices to those of the Uglies, and Manna lustily joined us with a resounding "Moondust!"

When Luna remained silent, Manna jabbed her wounded shoulder. "What's the matter, dear, the fox got your tongue?"

Rahab was quick to master her craft, to anticipate and exploit the sudden fierce gusts, the quick subsidings, which had doomed her predecessor. Whenever she banked or looped, she glittered redly between the pale green wings of her Moth. She seemed a part of the Moth; she did not control it, she became it. A Centaur is not a man riding a horse, but a horse-man, the two inseparable. It was the same with Rahab and her Moth.

No gratuitous acrobatics for her. She had a war to

win. I saw that she had slipped her feet from the stirrups and crept forward along the body to dip her craft at the Moth which was climbing under her. After mere seconds in the air, she was ready for a kill.

The Rider of the Moth—it was the Tiger—did nothing to avert a collision. She was simply allowing her craft to rise with the wind. Perhaps she had not yet mastered the intricacies of flight. Perhaps she expected Rahab to make room for her and then, on the same level, they would meet, circle, battle. But Rahab held to her dive. They would battle indeed, but she would choose their ground.

As a small child I had stood on a headland near Gournia and watched a Cretan galley drive down upon a Mycenaean invader. The moments before they met had seemed to pause instead of pass. I had had time in which to count the oars on both ships and observe that the Cretan carried a red half-moon painted on her prow. I had seen the look of—not fear, but fate—in the eyes of the opposing captains. In the instant before collision, the Cretan galley had veered, her own oars raised, and raked the side of the Mycenaen, snapping her oars like dry wheat stalks, crippling her, turning and returning to sink her with a bronze-beaked prow. It was much the same now. I could see the thongs in Rahab's boots. I could see the bracelet on the arm of her opponent.

Rahab, however, veered under rather than to the left or right of the Tiger Moth. At the same time she turned on her side, the tip of her wing almost grazing the Moth's belly. What was her purpose? A wing tip was not a prow! If anything, she would wreck her own craft. Then I saw that in passing she had used her slasher to sever the enemy's cord. The lower end whipped and twined like the body of a snake trying to recover its head. At first it was not apparent to the Rider of the Tiger Moth that she had lost her contact with the ground. It seemed to her only that Rahab had moved under her without inflicting damage. When her craft listed, we could see her face, first its puzzlement, then its unbelieving horror as she lurched upward and out of control toward the roof of the cave.

Zeb was punching my arm. "She's won, she's won!"

"There are still two to go," I said grimly, wondering how Rahab could endure another duel, much less two, when I who had merely watched her felt as if I had been swallowed and regurgitated by all six heads of Scylla and then thrown to Charybdis. My loincloth was sweat-wrapped around my thighs. I shivered with cold between the hot blasts of the Well. My voice sounded as if it were coming through moss and leaves in the bottom of a hollow tree.

"Only one now. One got it while Rahab was downing the Tiger."

The Emperor Moth, it seemed, had received a mortal wound. Its wings and its crowns were shredded; I recognized the work of a savagely applied slasher, the claw instead of the blade. It spun out of control and flung its Rider into the Well. The little girls with Ram squealed and flung their hands up to their eyes. Ram, though, watched without a sound. He was thinking with me: Moondust has only one opponent now.

That opponent was the Death's-Head Hawk Moth, whose Rider was even now steadying her craft for the final confrontation. She wore a tunic, armlets, and leggings of lapis lazuli, but neither sandals nor boots (it was she who had held her breath when she passed the Uglies on the third level). Probably she had hoped to limit her weight and increase her maneuverability. In the orange, magnifying light, I could see that she was smiling, and it seemed to me that all the envy and hatred which the less beautiful Wingers felt for the Comelies was contorted into that fixed, cruel smile. I thought: she is blue and silver ice. She can chill like snow or stab like an icicle. She will glory in killing, not in winning the War.

The Riders faced each other warily, circling the spout almost on the same level; each of them waiting, the blue and the red, killers by choice but for different reasons; waiting not for an error on the other's part— each had fought skillfully and knew the other's skill— but for a fluke of the wind, an air pocket, an updraft (the whim of a lost Rider?) to disconcert or immobilize the foe. And the fluke came like an unexpected wave, slapping Rahab's craft on the belly, hard, hard, and shivering it up the spout. For the moment, there was no question of guiding; it was enough for her to stay with the craft.

In that moment, the blue Rider duplicated Rahab's own tactics. Gliding under her, tilting, she flashed once, twice, quickly, decisively, with her slasher and severed Rahab's cord. Rahab had managed to balance her craft; her loss of control had been brief. But the spout held her now, lifted her almost lovingly, with slow liquid grace, toward the cavern roof and the downpointing stone trees.

I felt Zeb's arm around my shoulder. I clung to him with the desperation of the drowning, or rather of one who helplessly watches a drowning. For it was Rahab who needed an island. Zeb was strong for me, but who could help her in the islandless waters of the sky where the only shore was murderous with rocks? She had been a valiant warrior. Soon she would be a child's broken doll.

But the winds were whimsical. Having doomed her, they could afford to delay, to dally. For a second, no more, they held her motionless above the Death's-Head Moth. Was it sheer playful cruelty? Or perhaps—just perhaps—a flickering of conscience in one who had ridden like Rahab, who had died as Rahab was about to die? A gesture of admiration from a dead Rider to a live one: Here is a moment stolen from death. Endure it if you must; use it if you can.

Rahab used it. Her action was both simple and decisive. Arms held close to her, wings furled, she tipped her craft and rolled into the air. The Death's-Head Moth rose under her like the hand of a Cyclops and plucked her from the current.

The blue Rider was too astonished to act; she simply clung. She had won the War, so she thought, but here was her foe materialized beside her!

Rahab rolled against her and, kicking savagely, possessed the stirrup and most of the narrow Moth's back. The girl's hands continued to cling even after her feet lost their hold and her legs swung down to the far side of the back. But the Moth began to tip, Rahab was tipping it, and the hands trembled, the tightly curled fingers loosened and lengthened.

Arms outspread, scratching the air, she whirled away from her Moth to be crucified by the wind. We heard her scream. She sounded more surprised than frightened.

The Death's-Head Moth was starting to disintegrate.

The weight of two Riders had overburdened the wings; the ribs had begun to bend, the silk to rend. The Servitors on the ground were frantically winding the cord and trying to land the craft. Minutes were needed; seconds remained. But Rahab had shown that she could make a second work for her. With the last maneuver left in the faltering wreckage, she veered to the edge of the spout, whose hard winds enclosed her like the walls of a glass funnel. Using her boots to thrust, she kicked herself away from the Moth and against those walls, which cracked, parted, released her into the mild surrounding air: flotsam ejected by a waterspout.

The air no longer buoyed her. She began to fall. But Rahab had wings. The disused, largely atrophied wings which had born her ancestors over the desert sea, the wings which seemed to have become purely decorative and certainly incapable of sustaining flight, at least broke her fall. She fell in a fluttering spiral, fast but not fatally fast. She struck the ground hard, but feet first and cushioned by the boots. Bending her knees, she tumbled over and over, to lie at last on her face.

I was the first to reach her. She had landed on the terrace of the fennecs, who crowded around her with excited chatterings, but I kicked them out of my way—nasty creatures, overgrown rats—and reached her before she could move.

She turned on her back and smiled through dust and blood. Zeb was already beside her. He knelt and explored her body with his big, patient fingers. He looked up at me, serious but not solemn.

"She's badly bruised, but she hasn't broken any bones."

I lifted her in my arms and began to climb the terraces. No one got in my way, fennecs, Wingers, or humans. Zeb saw to that.

"Get a chariot ready!" I shouted to the Uglies.

"It was the boots," she said. "Your boots saved me."

"You had to know what to do with them."

"It was you who gave them to me. And everything else." She caught her breath. "They'll let you go now."

"I won't go without you. And Ram."

Anger clouded her eyes; lavender swirled to violet. "Do you think I fought so you could stay here and lose your manhood? You'll go back to Jericho. You and Zeb. I'll find a way to follow you. With your brother."

I felt immeasurably humbled by her valor—and her grandeur. I felt the limits to my own strength. I was not ashamed when I said:

"I'll go then. For your sake." It was the only gift which I could give to her.

Chackal was waiting at the top of the arena. He looked at Rahab closely as I lifted her into a yoked chariot. He was radiant. His Servitor, his Comely, had won the War. And she had not marred her loveliness.

X

"Hat, yes, but not the camel."

"The ostrich then?"

"Too tall."

"Love me, love my ostrich."

"I love you *and* your animals, but a two-room house has limits. Besides, what will they eat?" I was nursing a severe sunburn from our trek in the desert.

"Each other, if necessary. Here, rub some olive oil on your skin. It works wonders on goats with mange."

"They may prefer a change of diet. Two legs instead of four."

"Hat had her chance," he reminded me. "I thought she showed admirable restraint."

Yesterday we had returned from Honey Heart. True to his words, Chackal had released us after Rahab's victory in the War; he himself had conducted us—Zeb, Hat, and me—through a tunnel which opened at the foot of Jebel Kuruntul and we had made our hot and strenuous way across the desert to Jericho. He had indicated through Rahab, however, that he had not finished with us. Before our departure, she had said:

"I think he means to use your house as a kind of base. You know, the fennecs plan to infiltrate on a large scale. Don't be surprised if Chackal and some of his friends appear at your door. With Uglies."

"Suppose I didn't return to the house. Went to the Wanderers instead."

"He's considered the possibility. Remember he was with us the night we harbored the spies. He knows our sympathies. If you went to the Wanderers, he would punish me."

"Punish you? Even after your victory?"

"He feels he's more than repaid me by letting you go. If you go to the wrong place—to those he despises because they threaten his work in Jericho—he can think me pain. If he gets angry enough, he can will me to die. To stop eating. To stop breathing. But you have to realize, Bard, that I would *want* you to go to the Wanderers if there was any way you could help them. If Chackal punishes me—well, let him. I can take a little punishment—a lot, in fact, for the sake of Salmon's people. Or you. When Chackal's hold over you becomes unbearable, break it."

When we left her, Jericho had seemed more frightened than threatened by the Wanderers. First they must cross the Jordan, then they must scale or level a formidable ring of double walls. In the week of our absence, however, they had dammed the Jordan by tumbling rocks down from the cliffs above the banks and crossed with their entire company of warriors, women, children, and animals. According to reports in the town, several thousand tents crouched like big black spiders on the west bank; women sat weaving tunics for their men—bulky Simlahs would not do in a battle—and children played war games in which they built cities out of aspen branches and put them to the torch. The warriors—and all the grown men appeared to be trained for war—were striding through the oasis of Jericho, shaking coconuts from the palm trees and coming as close as they dared to the city walls without risking arrows from the Egyptian garrison.

The hardier farmers still ventured out of the gate in the morning and scurried back to shelter at night; an occasional caravan still departed for Ai or Jerusalem. All in all, though, the city had drawn in like a crab; unwounded but unwilling to risk wounds; making no threats but hard to crack. The Wanderers did not have to capture Jericho in order to advance into Canaan, but to leave such a city in their rear was to risk attack by the Egyptian garrison which, though puny at the moment, might later be strengthened by Egypt. It was general knowledge in Jericho that the Wanderers feared

144

and detested Egypt. It was generally agreed that they would besiege the city.

I had invited Zeb to share my house on the wall, since Rahab and I had been promised sanctuary for shielding the spies. He had begun to bring his animals from the temple.

"You know what soldiers do when they capture a city. Sacrifice the animals as hecatombs or else eat them." Already there were three goats and two pigs on the roof, all of them carried up the ladder by means of a hoist which Zeb had devised and which I, unfortunately, had helped to operate in the hot sun and at further cost to my arms and face. Odorous Hat, too self-indulgent to be trusted with the smaller animals, was settled in Rahab's room; asleep, if I could judge from the absence of padding feet, though her odor, a mixture of rancid milk and raw meat, issued through the door like one of those streamlets which run beside city streets and dispose of garbage.

I sat on the pallet in the front room and thought of Rahab. Rather, I allowed her to move from the back of my mind to blaze in the foreground: disobeying Chackal; stabbing Luna; winning the Wind War through craft and courage. Beloved Rahab. Imperiled Rahab. It had been pleasant to banter with Zeb about his animals; even to bemoan my sunburn; to forget, for the moment, that Rahab had not returned with us. But there were limits to forgetting.

"Zeb," I said. "How are we going to rescue her?"

"The ostrich?" he said happily, joining me on the pallet. "That's no problem. We'll blindfold her and then she can be led right through the streets to your house and kept in here with us."

"Rahab," I corrected.

"Well," he said, "we could always invade Honey Heart. If the Wanderers take Jericho, they might be willing to launch a second invasion. One conquest whets the appetite for another. That Salmon you mentioned, the one with the big feet, sounds like quite a warrior."

"And what would Chackal do to Rahab the minute we began the invasion? Besides, nobody's taken Jericho. There are still the walls, and the Wanderers don't seem to know the first thing about laying a siege. They appear to be waiting for advice from Yahweh, and he's a mountain god, not a city god. He's out of his element."

"Think of it this way. Rahab's happy because she saved you. The best way to keep her happy is to stay saved, at least for the moment. Don't go running back to Honey Heart on your own. Last time you almost ceased to be, as the Wingers would say, profitable. This time—"

Then we saw Chackal.

He was seated on his haunches inside the door. He looked as if he had not only had time to arrive and sit, to size up the room, to grow comfortable with possession, but also to eavesdrop on our conversation.

I jumped to my feet and seized a broom, a bundle of brushwood tied to a wooden cane. Whether I would have swatted him or swept him out the door, I am not sure. One thing I know. I meant to do him harm. When he saw my intention, he bared his teeth and cowered against the curtain.

Zeb caught me by the belt. "Hit him and he'll hurt Rahab."

I started to ask, "Suppose I killed him?" but mentally

I answered my own question: "Other fennecs would hurt Rahab."

"Make yourself at home, Chackal," I said. "But you already have, haven't you?" He was investigating the room, disdaining the red dust which blew from the desert and, in spite of the broom, had not been swept for days, admiring a clay figurine of a fennec which I had never been able to sell, coming at last, and with slow, deliberate grace, to the door into Rahab's room. It was a room with which he was intimately familiar. He entered with the air of a pharaoh visiting his favorite concubine.

"He's reminding us of his power over Rahab," I said. "In effect, he's claiming complete possession of the house for himself, his cronies, and no doubt an Ugly or two. Since he has Rahab, he can use her as a perpetual hostage. For the next twenty years, I'll be emerging Uglies and sending them out to profit."

"Sending them out? You'll be bringing them the wherewithal right here in your house!" He speculated. "I suppose I can help out if the demand exceeds the supply."

The noise I heard from Rahab's room was so muffled that it might have escaped my ears except for a lapse in our conversation as I envisaged my house transformed into a brothel. There was a yelp which could easily have been no more than a cough, a clearing of the throat. There was the slow, rhythmic motion of jaws, no more audible than the ruminating of a cow.

"What is Chackal finding to eat in there?" I asked. "Did you leave some meat for Hat?"

"No, but I left Hat."

"Then it isn't Chackal who's eating."

We raised the curtain.

"You really can't blame Hat," said Zeb quickly. "Not after what Chackal did to her. And me. Hyenas hold grudges, you know. They *bide*."

"I'm not blaming her," I said, speaking with difficulty. I did not know what to feel. I could not calculate the consequences. I only knew that precipitate action was required of me. "She thought she was doing us a favor. But Shin only knows what the fennecs will do when they find out. Zeb, I'm going to the Wanderers. Maybe they'll help me get Rahab out of Honey Heart. Maybe I can help them in return, as she hoped."

He looked as if I were about to forsake him. "Oughtn't you to stay here with me and explain things to the next fennec who comes?"

"Hat is impossible to explain. Why don't you come with me?"

"You know I want to come. There's nothing I want more. But I ought to stay with my animals. Be here with them if the city falls."

"When that happens, I won't let the Wanderers hurt you *or* your animals. Just don't take down the scarlet sash. In the meantime, there are some coconuts on the roof. Bread and cheese in the cupboard. Here are some silvers. I won't be needing them among the Wanderers, and you have extra mouths to feed, now that you've moved some of your animals out of the temple. If you run short of tunics, I'm leaving several in my chest. I know you prefer purple, but there's a green one you might like—"

"I can't wear your tunics," he said mournfully. "I'm too large for them." It was as if he had said: "I am losing my best friend." There were big tears in his eyes.

"Zeb, I'm just going to the west bank of the Jordan. That's only five miles. You know I'll be back."

"I don't know at all, and anyway, who's going to look after you?"

I almost protested: "Look after me? I can look after myself!" Instead, since it was Zeb: "I'll just have to make out on my own. Just for a little while, you understand."

I hugged him and felt momentarily as if I were wrapped in a bearskin coverlet, secure against the world.

Then, Joshua, I left Jericho and came to find you. It took me a whole day to get to your camp. Your scouts kept giving chase before I could explain what I wanted. I had to dodge three slingshots and a javelin. Finally, I stood on a hill and shouted: "I want to tell Joshua about Rahab, the woman with wings!" That did it. They put away their weapons and brought me right to you.

I came to ask your help.

The night had passed with my story, and morning ambered the roof of the tent until I could see the sp of gray in Joshua's beard.

He sat quiescent, like a mountain which may be volcanic. You are not sure if it will bask in the sun or erupt. Perhaps my story had sounded incredible to him. Rahab's wings he could accept; Salmon had doubt less told him about the "heavenly visitant." But the fennecs! I knew that the Wanderers had a high regard for womanhood, and the thought of women as Servitors to animals no bigger than cats would be repugnant to them.

His silent companions continued to crouch in his shadow like foothills. The woman who had taken a dislike to me had ceased to appear from and disappear into the adjoining chamber.

"What you have told me," said Joshua, spacing his words for emphasis and making a pronouncement instead of a statement, "is outlandish, not to say preposterous." He paused; I could hear the rumblings of the volcano. "True, we were warned by Moses that the Promised Land was not without its marvels. Its giants and other monsters. Even so, I doubt that I would have believed you had it not been for a particular circumstance—"

"Joshua, you *will* help me find Rahab, won't you? Get her out of Honey Heart? You could lead some men in there and clean out the place."

"One city at a time, my boy."

"But Rahab is in peril!"

He rose. You might almost say that he ascended, he was so tall. He took me by the arm in a gesture which was meant to be paternal but which was altogether terrifying—I felt sacrificial—and led me to a small black tent whose flaps were closed against the disturbances of morning.

"Here is the circumstance," he said, lifting a flap, placing it in my hand, and leaving me to my own discoveries.

Rahab was sleeping under a goatskin coverlet. Moondust, paragon of the Comelies, temptress of Jericho, slept like a shepherd girl on a bare hillside. There is a kind of beauty which needs no reflected luster from its surroundings, which burns with its own internal fires. Rahab, after all, was not of the moon, not the reflected light of a reflecting world. She was the sun's child; not Moondust but Sunburst.

She opened her eyes and smiled as if no worlds had ever thundered between us. As if she were waking to one who had the right to wake her.

"You see, I did follow you. And I brought your brother. He's in the next chamber."

He looked as if he had been wrestling with his goatskin. He was clutching the edge to his tangled curls.

"I'm not going to wake him," I said. "Not yet. He seems to have had a nightmare—and won. The fox isn't chasing him any longer."

I sat down on Rahab's pallet and held her hand, feeling like a boy with his first sweetheart, which of course I was.

"You were always a little afraid to touch me," she said. "First because I was ugly. Then because I was beautiful."

"It was because I looked on you as a sister."

"I never wanted to be your sister. I loved you from the first night in your house, when you protected me from your mother. But now I must tell you how I came here."

"By a miracle."

"By walking. Dearest Bard, when will you understand that I'm not in the least miraculous? When Chackal was killed, I knew at once. I felt his death in my thoughts. Even its circumstances. Pain, knowledge, and relief, all in a few seconds. I knew that the other fennecs would kill me when they learned what had happened. Some of them were planning to visit your house. I knew what they would find. I had to leave Honey Heart at once. I said that Chackal had summoned me. That he wanted me back in the house to prepare for the next arrivals. You know how fastidious they are. I said that the house was dusty and quite uninhabitable without a thorough cleaning."

"But Ram—"

"And I said that Chackal wanted Ram with me. The Jerichites would accept fennecs, Uglies, and Wingers far more readily as part of a human family. You, me, and Ram. What could seem more natural? They had no reason to suspect me. Why should they? It never occurred to them that Chackal might be dead. While he was alive, I could never make up such a story. They let me go. They even gave me a vial of nard to bring Chackal while he was Dirt-Going.

"I pretended to head for Jericho by way of the Hyksos ruin, but I left the main tunnels before reaching the city and came to the surface outside the walls. I found this camp without difficulty—you can't miss several thousand tents—and the Wanderers brought me right to Joshua. Salmon had told him about my wings. Joshua was very respectful. I could swear, though, that he still thinks I came from the heavens. Down instead of up. The direction of my coming goes against his notions of cosmology. He kept muttering that heavenly visitants don't come from Sheol."

"That's why he didn't tell me right off you were here. He wanted to see if our stories agreed. I must say that whatever these so-called visitants are, they must be extraordinary. I'm inclined to agree with Joshua. In your case, coming up is coming down."

"Are you calling me an angel?" She smiled. "That's the Wanderers' name for the visitants. But I'm not in the least heavenly."

"All I know of heaven is you," I said. "You and Ram and Zeb. It's all I want to know. But Zeb is still in the city. I hope the Wanderers can get him out."

"He won't come on his own?"

"Not without his animals, and the Jerichites would never let all that meat on the hoof escape them. Not when they're threatened by a siege."

"But the walls—can the Wanderers ever climb them?"

"I think," I said, with the suddenness of inspiration, "that there may be a way to dispose of the walls!" I was already on my feet. So quickly had the plan occurred to me that I had to ascribe it to Yahweh (who else? I was with his people).

"Joshua, *Joshua!*" I shouted, racing toward his tent.

I am sure that the mountain had never been summoned from his own tent by a mere anthill. He met me with good humor, though, and forestalled his guards from exercising their staffs.

I blurted my Yahweh-sent plan. "There are tunnels which lead under Jericho, as I told you last night. If some men could invade those tunnels, or rather a particular tunnel—" Here I removed a sandal and drew a map in the sand to indicate the one which led from Honey Heart to the Hyksos ruin, the one whose walls had been damp from their nearness to the Moon Stream. "They could break through the wall and the stream would flood that tunnel and all the adjacent ones. It would make the ground thoroughly sodden *under the east wall* of Jericho. Then with just a little pressure on the wall, battering rams—you don't have those, do you?—a mild earthquake—"

"A mild earthquake you say?" He looked speculative.

"We have them often in these parts."

"We couldn't wait indefinitely, of course. But earthquakes can be arranged, can't they? Minor ones, at least."

"With the help of a god like Yahweh, I'm sure they can. He's a god of mountains, which are made of earth. He surely knows how to move it about—quake it, as it were. And the double wall would come tumbling right down the hill and you could put the city to the torch—after you had rescued Zeb and his animals. Furthermore, the fennecs would lose their profiting grounds. All their plans, experiments, expenses—all their Dirt-Going—would come to nothing, and they would be well served for their mischief and their meddling."

"But who will invade the tunnel? You say it's entered from the Hyksos ruin. We're out here. As yet, the walls are keeping us here."

"But I can come and go as I please! No one stopped me when I left the city. Farmers still go into the fields and come back in the evening. Shepherds still lead out their flocks to pasture. I'll return to my house and get Zeb. We'll follow the same route we did before. Once in the tunnel, we'll let in a trickle from the stream and get out of there before it becomes a flood. Then we'll hurry back to my house on the wall—the north wall, which shouldn't collapse—and when you take the city, your men will see the scarlet sash and spare us."

"And I'll go with Bard," said Rahab. "Your men might overlook the sash in the confusion of battle. But no one can overlook my wings."

"The will of Yahweh moves in mysterious ways," said Joshua.

Now Jericho was straitly shut up because of the children of Israel: none went out, and none came in.

And the Lord said unto Joshua, See, I have given into thine hand Jericho, and the king thereof, and the mighty men of valour.

And ye shall compass the city, all ye men of war, and go round about the city once. Thus shalt thou do six days.

And seven priests shall bear before the ark seven trumpets of rams' horns: and the seventh day he shall compass the city seven times, and the priests shall blow with the trumpets.

And it shall come to pass, that when they make a long blast with the ram's horn, and when ye hear the sound of the trumpet, all the people shall shout with a great shout; and the wall of the city shall fall down flat, and the people shall ascend up every man straight before him. . . .

And the city shall be accursed, even it, and all that are therein, to the Lord: only Rahab the harlot shall live, she and all that are with her in the house, because she hid the messengers that we sent. . . .

Rahab, my wife of six months, had brought forth a son. Her friends had gathered with me outside her tent in the Wanderers' new encampment near conquered Ai. Gathered, I should add, with apprehensions as well as gifts. All of us knew that the sons of the Wingers were likely to be misshapen dwarfs who never outgrew their ugliness—Uglies who never emerged.

Zeb had come from his animals. He had made a triumphant return to his first profession. He was now the chief herdsman for all the flocks of the Wanderers, an aggregate of cows, sheep, and asses which had prospered and multiplied under his supervision, even though the incorrigible Hat, whom he had trained as a sheep dog, accompanied him on his rounds. Salmon, now the captain of a hundred men, had left them to practice the lethal uses of the slingshot and arrived with a justifiable if annoying air of ownership. Rahab and I had promised to make him the child's godfather; we felt obligated after his contribution. Finally, there was Ram, shorn to a trim little boy with a goatskin around his waist and a slingshot in his hand.

It was my own first sight of the child. The midwife, who seemed to feel that conceiving and bearing children was the sole accomplishment of women and that men, even husbands, were superfluous at any time and unendurable at this particular time, had kept me at bay till the child had been bathed, anointed with aromatic gum, and wrapped in swaddling clothes.

I took him from Rahab's arms and held him in front of me. The parts which showed were red, hairless, and distressingly plain. Both the midwife and Rahab looked as if they expected effusions. I was incapable of a stammer.

"He looks like a raw pork chop," Ram said. "Can't you swaddle the rest of him?"

"Pork chop indeed!" growled the midwife. "Doesn't that child know what Moses thought of pigs?"

"Ram meant to say lamb chop," I hurried to add. "But we'll love it anyway."

"But that's how all babies look at first," Rahab laughed. "He's quite normal, I promise. Abnormal, I should say, for a Winger's son. He'll grow into a fine man just like his—er—just like you, Bard."

"You're sure?" asked Ram. "He's made a poor start. He doesn't look at *all* like Bard."

Salmon hastened to agree with Rahab. "In fact, for his tender age he's the handsomest son I've ever—been godfather to. I'm sure he'll grow up to be a general with a wide following among the ladies."

Zeb was equally hopeful. "He's prettier than a new-born lamb."

Ram was convinced that he would become a pig farmer, Mosaic Law notwithstanding.

The midwife said, "Pity it wasn't a girl, but since it wasn't, he just might be an admiral since his father comes from Crete." At that, the men tactfully removed her, since her stance by the couch had begun to look permanent, and left me alone with Rahab.

"You know," I said, "even if he stayed this way—like a raw lamb chop—I would love him. I might even love him more than if he was beautiful!" I cradled him somewhat tentatively so as not to damage his head.

"Now you can do for," Rahab said.

"What?" I was wondering whether he would be a general, an admiral, or a pig farmer.

"You've always wanted to do things for people. To advise and manage them, for their own good, of course. It hurt you to have help from anybody, even when you were hardly more than a little boy. From me or Zeb."

"Or Salmon. You're right, it did hurt. I've had to be looked after all the way. Zeb and Hat led me to Honey Heart. You fought for me in the Wind War."

"But don't you see? You were the kind of person worth looking after. That made all the difference. And you learned to take help with a reasonably good disposition. Now you've earned the right to *give* help.

157

From now on. I think we're going to multiply like Zeb's herds, and you'll love each child more than the one before, and manage him beautifully."

"No. I'll love them all the same. I couldn't love them more than what's his name here."

"Boaz. The Wanderers say that means the Lord of Strength. Our Boaz will be strong in love."

"Boaz. I like the name. Somehow, I feel as if it's going to become famous."

ACKNOWLEDGMENTS AND NOTES

I wish to acknowledge with gratitude a large debt to the following books: *The Westminster Dictionary of the Bible, The Story of Jericho, Everyday Life in Old Testament Times, Everyday Life in Ancient Times,* and the King James Bible.

According to Biblical tradition, the Jerichite harlot Rahab (also called Rachab) was the mother of Boaz by the Israelite spy Salmon—the same Boaz who married Ruth and became the ancestor of both David and Christ. The tradition does not say that Rahab married Salmon, however, and I have taken a fantasist's liberty of inventing a different husband for her.

My occasional references to beings from Greek mythology—Cyclops, Scylla, etc.—are made under the assumption that these beings may have come to the Greeks through their Cretan heritage. Thus, my hero from Knossos would be familiar with them.

THOMAS BURNETT SWANN was born in Florida in 1928 and served in the U. S. Navy during the Korean war. His education includes an A.B. from Duke University, Master's from the University of Tennessee and Ph.D. from the University of Florida; he is presently an English professor at Florida Atlantic University, the nation's first Senior College. In addition to his fantasy and science-fiction, he has published books of literary scholarship (*The Classical World of H.D.; Charles Sorley, Poet of World War I;* etc.) as well as poetry (*Wombats and Moondust; Alas, in Lilliput*). He has traveled extensively, doing research for both his nonfiction and fiction

His previous Ace Books include:
    DAY OF THE MINOTAUR
    THE WEIRWOODS
    THE DOLPHIN AND THE DEEP